100
WAYS THE
WORLD ENDS

100 Ways the World Ends

by Jim Marcus

May 2025

This book is set in Lato Regular 9/13
Titles in Lato Heavy 16/20

Cover:
The End

by Jim Marcus 2025

ISBN 979-8-9924718-2-3

Chapters

■ ।। PULSEBLACK ।।

12:33 ।।- 90 18 ।- 4:

83

by XENOX®

Dedicated

To my kids, Mission, Donna, and Coda, who are the future, there is a little of each of you in this.

....

"The secret of our success is that we

never,

never give up."

-Wilma Mankiller

1 Tinmiaq

I used to fly just to be in the air.

Before all that - before all this, I was a pilot. I had my license when I was fifteen. My mom was a pilot, too. She used to talk about how she'd met my dad on a quick charter flight that he wasn't dressed nearly warmly enough for, and all she wanted to do was to hug him and warm him up. And maybe smack him for not having the good sense to bring a sweater to a flight over Ottawa.

After that came another flight. And then one more before they fell in love. Leading into twenty years of happiness until he passed away, after one beautiful child, if I say so myself, and a good, solid life together, laughing in the kitchen while learning new recipes, screaming loudly at their daughter's volleyball games, teaching the neighbor kids how to swim and sneaking off to fly, whenever they could, to tiny Ottawa private airports peppered with little personal planes held together with bondo, duct tape, and hope.

And after years together, my mom became ever more and more thankful that she had flown that first charter flight with that smiling Nigerian man in his thin short sleeved shirt and sandals. And that she hadn't actually reached over to slap him.

Besides, you need two hands to fly.

And even if you're not the one in that seat, it's probably a good idea to keep two hands free.

I was leaning against the cold metal of the Ting trying to quiet my brain a little and maybe not fall over. Ladia, Ella, and Herman were right in front of me. The sky was exploding, threatening to take our pretty little winged metal box with it. Ladia looked at me, bit her lip, and pointed to the back where a younger airman with a shock of black hair had vomited against the far wall of the plane.

I inhaled, "Dempsey, are you going to be ok?"

He straightened up and looked forward, "Yes, sir, Just trying to keep lunch down."

"Understood." I winked at Ladia, "Two points for noticing that lunch sucked and so does this. So, just keep paying attention and you'll be fine."

I could actually hear a few chuckles behind me over the bombing. It was a victory.

Dempsey smiled, "You got it, Colonel."

The Ting shook with the aftershock of artillery placed entirely too close. We were fast, but not invisible…

Or invulnerable.

You're probably guessing at a few things. For a 32-year-old to be a Colonel after only ten years of active military duty, two things must be true:

She has to be at least moderately good at what she does.

A lot of people ahead of her must be dead and the war is not going well.

Out of modesty, I can't speak to the former. I joined the military because we did good work. We built things people needed. We brought food to people who lived where the food wasn't. We helped mediate problems between peoples who didn't see a peaceful outcome. And for six years, that was my job and my life. I traveled, I made friends, really good ones. And except for training and time at the range, I never touched a gun.

And even now, it felt heavy, cloddish, on my hip. It felt like carrying around some washed up piece of iron curving up against me that had no real purpose - just for show, just to prove I had one.

Then, impossibly, war came to us. It snuck over the border in the middle of the night and pretended it had always been there with a ferocity and a power that I couldn't have imagined. So many people died so quickly. We weren't prepared for the rhetoric to turn to violence so fast and they knew it. The border between the US and Canada is almost 9,000 kilometers and it represents the longest contiguous land border between any two countries in the world.

Overnight it became the biggest war front in history. And the alliance between the US and the newly reformed Soviet Union meant that they had the manpower to staff that border with throwaway infantrymen, both American and Soviet, to confront us from the side as well.

I'm not sure if I can emphasize how unexpectedly suddenly all this happened. I think a lot of writers who write history books try to foreshadow and elevate anterior information so that it all makes sense to the reader. They try to make it sound understandable to history students that the assassination of the archduke Ferdinand, for example, could, eventually, plunge the entire world into chaos or how a sitting president lightly mocking a failed businessman and TV personality at a correspondent's dinner, could cause him to organize the resources and foreign connections needed to run for president, win, and rip that nation apart like a private capital firm would an old rug company.

Canada went, overnight, from being a friendly neighboring nation to, somehow, the biggest threat to American sovereignty. And maybe we didn't respond quickly enough. Who's to say? The US has managed to, historically, paper its cage sufficiently to forget things like "A country that has never paid reparations for anything" and "a wealthy country whose land and labor were both stolen." Oh, and, in case it ever became relevant, "the only nation to use atomic weapons in warfare."

And it did.

Strategic Nuclear launches eliminated key military leadership which is how someone like me made her way to Colonel so quickly. And why I was on the air now. Trying to provide ground support to beautiful places, places I remembered as a kid, that weren't really places anymore.

But there were still people.

As another bomb wracked the plane, I looked over at Ladia. She'd been my best friend since way before basic training, and the four of us, Me, Ladia, Ella, and Herman, had been stationed together over and over. Ladia was a smart and quick half Dominican girl from Ottawa. I was probably the only one here who knew how pretty she looked in a dress, her long black hair let down. But everyone knew she could speak harder than any soldier.

Ella was from here, too, cool, easy going, covered in tattoos, her tightly curled hair pulled up high into an afro ball above her head while we shared inuk phrases designed to make guys go crazy over too many drinks in basic training.

And Herman was like everyone's Uncle – short white hair he'd had since he was thirty over a lined but beautiful face that was a constant host to some sort of a grin. No one didn't like Herman. But they still shot at him.

Like they did all of us. But, somehow, we survived.

I can't tell you for sure how that had happened, because it seemed unlikely as hell to me, too. But I wasn't lying to Dempsey. If you pay attention to your body, it will pay attention to details.

And right now, my body isn't saying anything good. It was telling me that this was a familiar situation. And situations like this happen.

And that the plane was pitching.

"Did you feel that?" Herman looked up. He was trying to pay attention to his body, too.

Ella grabbed the wall next to me, "The nose is dipping."

"Fuck." She was right. The plane bobbed as I made my way to the cockpit.

"It's locked."

Ladia detached from the wall and fell toward me. She pulled out her gun and placed two shots directly into the lock to the cockpit. I raised my boot and smacked it against the lower center of the door. It cracked off immediately and dropped into the tiny room.

"Sonafabitch." Ladia saw the faces of the strangled pilots as she aimed at the Redtop against the far wall of the cockpit. I could see the stick was dropping and the nose of the plane was dipping, pulling us down.

Redtop was in his early twenties, male, black. In today's America, acts of service to the state were ways that Black men could earn their way to citizenship- to being people.

I put my hands up and looked at him. He was holding a trigger in his left hand. "If you shoot me, the plane goes up."

"It's ok," I showed him my hands. "No one wants to shoot you."

"You do, she does, you want to kill us all."

"I do, actually," Ladia waved the gun.

"No, she doesn't want to shoot you. I just want to get in that seat so we all don't die."

"Bullshit," He pointed the trigger at me like a gun. I took a deep breath.

"Look, My name is Tomi Pinga. I'm a pilot. I can land this thing and then you can disappear."

"That's not my job." He looked me up and down.

And I did the same with him.

"Let me shoot him and let's do this." Ladia stage whispered at me. Everyone could hear that.

"I heard that," he mumbled.

"I know, the whispering was an effect." Laddia kept the little red dot steady on his forehead.

"What is your name?" I nodded at the Redtop. Nodding feels affirming to people. It triggers something.

"You don't care." The plane was falling faster now. I didn't have much time.

"I do care. I mean, you don't want to be doing this. You're an artist, right? A musician. You're about that beat, right?"

He looked at Ladia and then back at me, "Yeah, I'm a drummer, how did you know that?"

"If you let me stop this plane from crashing, I'll tell you."

"Let her land the plane, man. See? Look. " Ladia put down her gun.

He nodded and I pulled the co-pilots body from the seat. This still put one seat between me and the redtop. I fit myself into the seat and wrapped the seatbelt over my shoulder. The stick was like lead but I lifted it, and the nose lifted, too.

I don't want to think about how little margin that was.

"How did you know I was a drummer?"

"You look homeless," Ladia shot back.

"Ha. Very funny, bitch." He wasn't playing.

I tried to muster up all the soothing tone I could, "Well, your left hand is dominant, you've been holding that in your dominant hand. So,it's likely you are an artist of some kind. You're young, I guess. But you also seem to be capable with your other hand, like you spent time building lateral autonomy, plus you've been tapping nervously with your right foot. In time. Your forearms are larger than your upper arms, so I'm guessing you play jazz or r&b or something."

"Fuck."

"Now you tell me something. How did you end up here? I slid one hand into my pocket, texting Herman. If there was a bomb on board this plane, I needed to know everything about it.

"This is what we have to do. Most Canadians want this."

"That's bullshit, man. Those videos you see are altered." Ladia harrumphed.

I'd seen them as well. AI deep fake videos showing Canadians protesting to become America's 51st state.

"Bullshit." This seemed to be his default.

"What's your name?" I asked, looking for space to land.

He just shook his head.

"Can you at least tell us where this bomb is?" He held tight to the deadman's switch in his hands. In his mind, this was his insurance that he wasn't going to be shot. He probably wasn't wrong but I really wanted this to go a different way.

Herman poked his head in the cockpit. "We don't have a ball, Colonel. But everyone back here is ok."

"Thanks, Herm. Eyes up."

"Yup. I see you made a new friend." Herman shook his head in the Redtop's direction.

"I did. But we're going to go our separate ways once we get this crate down, right, Rhythm machine?"

He looked down and grumbled. I tried to keep his mind off the bomb.

"My manners. This is Hermann. He's a musician, too. He plays bass, right Herm?"

"I do love it. Standup. What's your name, man?"

"Look, shut the fuck up. I'm thinking"

"Ok. ok. Herm, let everyone know it's all good, ok?"

"Yes Sir, Colonel." He backed out.

The Redtop looked at me. His eyes were deep and black and they seemed to float in desperation. His hair was cropped close under the bright red hood he wore, indicative of the US civilian militias, people who had just gone out and bought a red Gildan cotton hoodie and tucked the hood until they needed to "act." No training, no support from the government, just constant reminders from a president over social media that they were heroes and whatever they did as civilians would be forgiven.

The schools were dry runs. For decades, men and boys like this would be inundated with the message that schools were sources of indoctrination, that they were there to make them feel stupid. And they were told the answer to their problems, all of them, was a gun, a weapon....

An explosion.

And afterward, the message was always the same. No one would stop them. No one would stop the next one.

Or the next one.

Can you have an army without a chain of command, without titles, without rank, without rules, without form? America was trying to show the world you could.

And this man was proof.

"You're a colonel?"

"I am." I leaned over and pushed the pilot's body from the seat. I was hoping I could get him to take some ownership of the plane. He looked back and forth between me and Ladia and slid into the seat. "Do you know the name of this plane? What does it mean?"

He shook his head.

"It's the Tingmiaq. It means 'bird' in Inuktitut. It's good luck. Do you know what an Inuit is?"

He shook his head again.

Inuits are a group of people native to this area. Some places in the US, too. And Inuktitut is one of the languages they speak.

"Sounds fucked up."

"Well, my last name is Pinga.

"She's a fucking goddess," Ladia interjected.

"I am. Pinga is the goddess of the hunt" I leaned over to him, "And the sky, lucky for me."

He actually smiled at me. I was getting close. I could be getting through to him.

"You look black, like me." He offered.

"I am. My dad was Nigerian. Probably from the same place your ancestors came from. My mom was an inuit. Her family lived here for thousands of years."

"He's done a lot for Blacks." The Redtop rattled off.

"Oh, yeah?" I wasn't anxious to bring this into politics, but I did want to keep him talking. "Tell us about it."

"You don't care. She doesn't." He pointed back at Ladia.

She rolled her eyes, "I do."

"I know you don't really want to hurt anyone. I have some scared people there. Can you tell us where the bomb is?"

"The bomb, on the plane?"

"Yeah, we can put that behind us and talk." I offered up.

He laughed, "You think there's a bomb on the plane?"

I was approaching the airfield. I only needed a few minutes. I tried to keep him talking so he wouldn't notice the descent. The radio was blinking furiously.

"That's what the dead man switch is for, isn't it? A bomb."

He looked at me and his face suddenly came alive. "There's no bomb on the plane. You stupid sheep bitch."

"What are you talking about?"

"These planes. All of them. Most are made in America. There's no bomb on the plane. The bomb IS the plane. And it's going to go off no matter what."

"Shit. Herman?!"

He peeked his head in, "Get everyone off. Now. I can't land this thing if it's a full-on bomb." Ladia holstered her gun and grabbed his hand with both hands.

"Let me go."

"Look, dick, you're lucky I didn't cut that hand off and shove it up your ass." She pulled his hand up and, from the corner of my eye I saw his red hoodie lift up and the gun in his waistband drop to the floor.

"Gun!" I yelled out as it slammed to the metal floor of the cockpit and went off, sending a bullet straight upward, through Ladia's neck and into the far wall. The plane bucked as the cabin decompressed and Ladia fell over. The Redtop dropped to the ground while the switch followed in the other direction, skittering across the floor and up against the nose of the plane.

The back of the plane exploded , pushing us all forward. I could feel the raw hot fringe of the wind through the cabin door as I looked down to see fountains of blood pouring out of Ladia's neck from her carotid artery, painting the floor of the cockpit in thick viscous red.

I tried to keep the plane from spinning, but I could only hold tight to the stick and watch us spiral toward the ground. Blood inched toward my boot as I yelled out to Ladia to hang in there, to hold on, thinking that all of this, too, felt familiar.

All this, too, felt like something that happened.

And then we caught fire.

.

2 - Ionia

In Ionia, you wake up every morning with a three digit number facing your bed, illuminated in the corner of the wall. Nobody really knew how they determined your health while you slept, or even what number was too low to work, but we all knew that, in a work camp like this, we needed to keep our health up or be eliminated. The number was a mercurial warning, just vague enough to keep you constantly on edge, just illuminating enough to give you something to strive for.

Today, my number read "981," which seemed higher than I felt, honestly. I assumed this was good, since there were only 3 numbers. The highest would have to be "999." Although, this was the kind of logic that could only get you in trouble in Ionia, I thought.

Up is down here.

I grabbed a shirt and wandered to the showers. By the time I made it to breakfast, there was no food left. I sat down with a thud on the round metal stool next to Ladia who started to assemble a plate for me from her own.

"Damn, girl. you're lagging today. You ok?"

"I was thinking about the Ting." I reached down and shoved a formless piece of random meat into my mouth.

"Yikes. Pass." She lifted her head and showed me the mark on her neck. I pulled her over and kissed it playfully as one of the red shirt guards shouted out. No affection.

"Sorry." I was starving now. I put a forkful of creamed powdered yellow stuff in my mouth. "So what do you think about, then?"

Ladia pointed across the room toward the girl. She was a beautiful dark-skinned Black girl with long dark hair, arrayed across her head in braids. She had one of those bodies that made the pajama-like formless work camp grey clothing look appealing. "I think about sex with her."

"So, wait, you HAD sex with her?"

"Well. I am a lady, so…" She took a drink of some unidentifiable juice and waved at her. She smiled and waved back, bouncing a tiny bit in place.

"Well. You're SHAPED like a lady. I'll give you that." Ladia was beautiful. And it wasn't just me who thought so. Men and women fell for her left and right. And then she would open her mouth and a stream of beautiful crazy would come out. You had to be this tall to ride that ride.

She leaned in. "So what does your guy say?"

I took a breath,"My guy says be ready at any time today. Or tomorrow. Bad sign being he didn't know today's date when I quizzed him."

She shoved something unidentifiable into her mouth. What the fuck were we eating here? "Lucky for you people I'm always ready. Except right now at this moment I feel a bit bloated. And ready. Bloated and ready."

Shimmy pulled up and slammed herself down right across from me. Shimmy was a larger woman, with close cropped blonde hair and a slight weight lifting addiction. I liked her. She wasn't military or even Canadian and I never did figure out what she was doing here. "Pinga, did you bet the guards that this place was going to explode today?"

"I shook my head, "No, no. I bet them that it wouldn't."

Ladia looked puzzled, "why would you do that?"

"Because I think this place is going to explode today and they'll think twice about killing me if I owe them money."

Shimmy stared at me. "Oh my god. I think I love you. You're fucking crazy."

Ladia tossed her a sausage shaped block of protein and asked the big question, "ok, Shimmy, before we're all dead, last chance. Tell us what you're doing here."

"Yes, Simco..." I asked, using her actual surname, "What is a happy go lucky American non military woman doing here in a prisoner of war camp near the Canadian Front?"

"You want to know? What's it worth?"

"Did you Tubman a bunch of Migrants into Quebec?" Ladia leaned forward conspiratorially.

"I wish it were something that cool. And I don't speak french."

I sighed, "This is the last mystery of Ionia I actually give a shit about, so fess up, Shimbolina."

She leaned in and whispered, "Are you guys actually leaving today?"

I shrugged and glanced at Ladia. "Who knows? We can't stay here forever. Last chance to decide if you want to come with..."

"I'm not a fighter. I mean, I look like one." She flexed. The rack of muscles hiding under her flab roared to life and stretched out across her arms and chest."

"That's no lie." Ladia was clearly impressed.

"Besides, someone needs to stay back here and make sure they don't hurt anyone."

"Promise me you'll take care of yourself, Shimmy?" We touched fingers, ignoring the guard's response from across the hall.They could go fuck themselves.

"You just worry about getting the fuck out of here," she smiled.

"Well, We'll miss you, you giant pumped up bitch." I watched her face light up as an alarm sounded out, low and caustic.

"That's one I haven't heard before." Ladia leaned over.

On cue, the guards had lost interest in us. Almost in unison they turned their backs to us and faced outward, arraying themselves at doorways and outside walls, their red shirts creating a kind of picket fence wall. The alarm was an external threat.

"I don't think that's for us."

Is that our ride?" Ladia called out. She followed me and shimmy as we tried to warn people over, away from the far wall.

I was about to lose a bet.

Suddenly the room exploded with hot kinetic expulsions of air, metal pieces, and plastic all around us. We dropped below the table line and prisoners all around the room followed suit. The light in the room died and the persistent hum of the generators died with them, leaving an eerie loss in that grumbly sonic space that had been so ubiquitous we barely noticed it anymore.

"God, this place is so much better in the dark, all blown to shit," Ladia shouted.

I shrugged, in the universal gesture of "Don't get used to it." and waited for it to hit my eyes as we shouted out "Carol-Anne" across the room.

And then, like water from a broken pipe, everyone in the room ran at once, into the light pouring across the room from the massive hole in the far wall. I grabbed Ladia's hand and positioned us both in the center of the wave full of people who'd seen Poltergeist at least once.

A lot of people.

I lost track of Shimmy and kept moving forward. The light hit our eyes, blinding us, so we just pushed on. Bullet trails snaked out all around us as the guards tried to keep everyone inside. After about fifty steps we had breached the wall and the light was now everywhere.

The tide of prisoners had become a spray hose, scattering everywhere, with guards chasing larger groups.

Luckily, we knew where we were going.

"Volleyball Court?" Ladia yelled out over the chaos. Ladia and I had our own code names for every part of the prison, named after what we wished were there. The hot tub was west. Tennis was in front. And the Volleyball court was directly east of the mess building.

"Yep." I pulled left and around the building and we saw it.

The Fearless.

It was huge, stretching out across the fence it had rammed. It must have been six or so meters wide and fifteen or sixteen meters long, with a lower part that looked like a grey tank and an upper area that was composed of connecting grey and yellow thick metal pods. It looked indestructible.

And my contact, Rey, was at the open door waving us on.

Rey was tall, Black, and English, with tightly curled short cropped hair and a pressed grey military shirt indicative of the British reserves. None of my communication with him had been verbal but I was fairly sure there was a thick English accent behind that square jaw. He was far better looking than he needed to be since he was rescuing me from a prison work camp.

But it was the Fearless that Ladia and I were running to.

It was beautiful. It was freedom.

We dodged bullets from the guards and tried to hug the ground as we advanced. It occurred to me that they might be pissed about me leaving while owing them money. It could have gone either way.

I guess that's why they call it gambling.

We slid into the open door and Rey slammed it shut almost too fast to see. It was bright inside, nearly as bright as in the yard, outside. It was far roomier than I thought with a big triage bay and a couch to my right. We fell onto the couch and the machine lurched forward.

I looked up at Rey who was kneeling down, checking us out. "We're good. Not hit. How many volts can this thing handle?"

Rey stood up, "Oh, the fence. The tracks are rubber, we're pretty safe."

Ladia looked up, "this fence is class E - about 20,000 volts. Can we do that?"

Rey scrunched his face up. "That is a lot."

I nodded affirmatively. "I say yes." I could hear the chaos around us and I wanted to get out of here before they found something that could pierce this thing. "Where is the driver?"

Rey palmed the wall and a door to my right slid open. All these doors were hyperfast for clearly understandable reasons. And they all sunk into the walls. That was smart. I liked this thing.

Rey slid into the Nav pod. "This is Symone. She's my second."

""Welcome aboard." She began to salute.

I waved my hand. "Good to be here. Do you think we can hit this fence and drive laterally along it until we take down the whole Southern face?"

"I say, Fuck that fence." She put both hands on the controls and pushed the stick forward. Once this whole fence was down, the guards will have more problems than just us, problems that would likely scatter in all directions. I looked at Rey and he nodded. I tucked myself into a seat next to Symone. The Nav pod took up half the width of the machine and it was airy and actually smelled good.

"Damn, This space here is bigger than my whole cell."

"It's over 3 by 4 meters. Room for backseat drivers." She smiled at me.

"Alright. I'll copilot this bitch."

"That's right. You're a bigshot pilot, too. I'll see if I can get this up to speed for you." One gear up and it seemed like we were moving even more smoothly. Faster than I would have expected.

"Symone," I leaned in, "I feel at home already."

Ladia leaned into the Nav Pod. I could tell she was impressed with the whole operation. The British were on their shit today.

Rey started, "Well, You know me. You've been talking with me. I'm Captain Avila. I've been the lead EMT and UN rep on this boat."

I could see out the front that we were destroying the fence. Lightning bounced off the Fearless all around us on the outside. I kept my eyes open, looking for problems while Rey spoke.

"This is Lieutenant Symone Garrison, second paramedic. And you, Colonel Pinga, are now ranking officers on the ship, while Lieutenant Arrakis, as an RN, is now ranking medical officer."

"Thank you for that rundown." This seemed to be a naval operation, I noted. And the Fearless itself had the Nav Pod on the left side, meaning it was made for North America. I filed that information away.

"We can play this as a field operation and dispense with salutes. I'm not super high protocol, so if anyone has good ideas, yell 'em out. I'll get the grand tour when we see this place behind us. Anyone else on deck?"

Symone looked up at Rey. Except for her shorter mop of dark black hair, she could have been my sister. It reminded me that I did need to dye my tips again. Rey looked awkward, "We have to pick up our engineer. Of course, right after we get your surgeon."

"That's right." I looked over at Ladia. "Let's go get our girl."

She kicked her feet and cheered.

It might take the British a bit to get used to us.

***

To explain why Ella was at a different prison, I first have to explain how fascism works.

In a fascist system, like America had become so quickly, nothing is more important, they say, than efficiency. Efficiency is the excuse to do nearly anything. And to get to efficiency, you need to categorize and classify EVERYTHING. Races need to be codified. That makes it possible to make decisions on which are superior. Mixed race people fuck up that narrative. So let's pretend they don't exist, they say. Or invent bizarre, arcane rules for how many drops of blood you can have and how dark your skin is and what shape your nose is.

Women must be treated very traditionally. Fascism considers women to be inefficient. They are compassionate and capable of seeing the world as interconnected. They are dangerous. They love their children more than the state.

And that's a no no.

Women need to be tamped down. Women need to be managed. So it's efficient to have a hard line between male and female. The problem is that this line does not exist. Gender is a continuum and so is biology. Ask someone one day why they stopped genetic testing at the Olympics. As well, when it comes to cultural gender expression, it's a pure, smooth continuum, all of which messes up the binary thought model that fascism needs to exist.

So one of the very first things all fascist regimes have to do is to eliminate trans people, to clear them from history, to press them back into binary molds.

To wipe them out.

And you can't find a fascist regime in history that hasn't started there.

Because of recently passed American anti-transgender legislation, Ella, a lieutenant in the Canadian Medical services, a surgeon, one of the leading transplant experts in north America, with a gun range score so poor that I had to forge it to even get her on my team, was a bigger threat than myself or Ladia.

Because she was intersex and didn't conform to their efficient models. And she belonged in a high security men's prison.

"Honestly, I'm offended that they put her in higher security than me." Ladia had pieced through the guns and found one she loved. She was cleaning it in the front triage area, leaning forward on the couch. For a nurse, she was a deadly shot.

Rey applauded, "That was the fastest I've ever seen that gun assembled."

"See. I'm dangerous. I could take Ella any day."

"I feel like I should wind this conversation down before we get her."

"For her sake, right? You don't want her to feel sad, right?"

I looked up at Rey, "Are you up to break into prison number two today?"

He was organizing papers half-heartedly. "The last time I was in America, I went to Disneyland and waited in lines all day. So, yes. Yes, I am."

"Exactly. I love your attitude."

Suddenly, Symone slammed the brakes and slid the door open. "Abandon ship!"

Rey turned to the starboard bay, the one we'd come aboard on, and palmed it. It quickly swung open and we poured out.

I pulled my gun out as we all made our way to the port side of the Fearless. There, in the direct center, was an object. It looked like a large bug.

"Ok, ew, what is that?" Ladia was aiming at it. I put my hand on the gun and slowly lowered her arm.

"Any ideas?" I hadn't seen anything like it before.

"It just registered on the internal sensors. I think they stuck it on us at the prison." Symone cocked her head. "I feel like it's familiar but I can't place it."

"Do we think it's a bomb?" Rey asked.

It seemed like it had to be. "Maybe a tracker? But it's huge for that." I pondered for a second. "It's not ticking. It's not doing anything.

Symone picked up a large rock. "Watch this." She threw the rock so it sailed over the top of the Fearless, right over the device. The scarab-like piece of machinery began to hum and glow. After a moment or so, it stopped.

"Ok," I concluded, "a proximity motion sensor."

"I guess it was building up energy as we drove." Symone wiped her hands off.

I looked at Rey, "Let's assume it's a bomb. Do we think the bomb can break through the hull?"

"Well, They thought so, or they wouldn't have bothered." Rey looked worried. I might be in charge right now but this ship was his. Or I'm sure it felt that way.

"Rey, say you all stand back. I approach this thing slowly and stop at intervals so it can't build. Then I quickly remove it. Does that sound reasonable to you?"

"That sounds insane to me." He shook his head. "But reasonable."

I took a step. And then another. I tried to remember the tone when Symone threw the rock. As long as I kept its hum under that tone, I should be fine, right?

I took another one. It buzzed a little, starting to hum. Each time I stopped. I turned slowly to look back.

Ladia had her head in her hands. Rey began to lead them to the other side. Better they didn't see this anyway.

I was just a meter away. It began to hum. I paused, paralyzed, before the device. My plan was to quickly dislodge it once it stopped humming, cognizant of my stillness.

But it kept building. My heart was beating to break out of my chest. I suddenly realized that I was close enough that my heart was triggering it. It was going to use that to go off. I turned quickly and began to run as the hum built in intensity.

And a wave of hot air hit me like a knife, splitting my body in half.

I fell face up and saw the hull of the fearless. There wasn't a scratch on it.

Before I fainted, I saw my body ripped in two, bleeding on the ground.

And I closed my eyes.

***

"See. I'm dangerous. I could take Ella any day." Ladia was assembling and cleaning her gun with a big smile on her face.

We were back on the Fearless. I was in one piece.

"Wait a second?"

Rey looked over, "are you ok?"

"Did you guys just experience anything?"

Rey cocked his head. "We're about to experience prison number two today."

"Stop the fearless. Now."

Symone slammed on the brakes while Ladia looked at me. She was ready for anything. I opened the door and moved to the port side, the rest following. On the hull was the scarab that had just exploded.

Symone looked up, "what the fuck is that?"

"I moved them all back. It's a proximity bomb. Does anyone remember seeing one of these?"

Rey shook his head. No one but me remembered what just happened.

"So what do we do?" Ladia lifted her gun.

I reached for her gun, "here. Cover your eyes." I lifted it and shot the device directly in the center. It exploded harmlessly.

Rey looked impressed, "Shit. no damage to the hull at all."

I handed Ladia back her gun. "Yeah. It was only a threat to one of us. They didn't realize how thick this thing was."

"How did you know that?" Symone lowered her voice and looked at me.

"Honestly…" I tried to decide what to say. I failed, just shrugging. "Let's just go get our girl."

Ladia cheered and jumped in the air.

As we piled back into the Fearless, I tried to reconstruct what had just happened. Either I was going insane or time was.

And I didn't like either of those options.

3 - Fearless

Rey gave me a tour of the Fearless.

The large area we had entered into was meant to be the only real public area of the ship. No civilians were allowed past it. It was called the "triage zone" and it was as wide as the Nav pod, about 3.5 meters, and long. It was about 8 meters long. One one side was the big couch area, with belts to strap in, and on the other, a sink, in front of a small bathroom and shower. Most of the triage areas I had ever worked in had been in helicopters and this was much larger. And having a sink right there along with a hygienic area would be a godsend, I bet.

It held a number of cots. And more could be expanded from the wall. And right where it met the hull was a medical storage area with a sort of lazy susan that dispensed medication. Most of the storage on the Fearless was arranged around the outside, protecting the people within. But also making it possible to jettison storage if needed. This seemed smart and very focused on crew integrity, which I liked a lot. These UN built vehicles were very focused on keeping the people inside alive and, as a person inside, well, I approved.

Against the inner wall, between Triage and the Nav pod, was an internal storage area for very important things. This was where many of the weapons were kept. A doorway led to the Nav area and one portside in the nav area led outward while another, behind, led to the Laboratory.

The lab was about 5 meters long with a miniature clean room in the back.

The hull wall opened to chemical storage. Behind that was the center corridor, with general storage for materials, finds, etc.

And this led to the living area in the back.

The kitchen, dining and lounge area were fairly spacious. We'd probably spend a lot of time here. I hated how far it was from the Nav pod, but that was more a security issue than anything. And we could override navigation from the kitchen. You could, if necessary, drive it from back here.

From there, it all led back to a 6 person bedroom, bathroom, and shower facilities. It was tight, but compared to Ionia, it was the Waldorf. The floors were all sleek black rubber and the walls clean metallic grey and white. It felt fresh and new.

And it was.

"So, this was made specifically for North America," I asked Rey, falling into the couch in the back lounge.

"You're right. There are twenty-four of these in existence. All Terrain Amphibious Rescue and Support Vehicles. (ATARAS). This is the Fearless, ATARAS-17 and it's all yours.

"Proof that the UN isn't abandoning North America." I mused.

"Oh, North America is a shit show. No doubt. The United States' alliances with Russia and North Korea will eventually lead to a complete takeover. Every second they spend pursuing America's war will be taken right out of America's hide. The best we can do is to be strategic and help the people of Canada survive and thrive any way we can."

"And to do that, we need to get some things in the US?" I looked over at Ladia.

"Yes, unfortunately. It's going to be complicated." Rey didn't seem happy about it.

Ladia asked the question before I did. "Are we authorized to be in the US?

I mean, at all?"

"Nobody is."

"Well, I feel special now. Why are we taking so long?" Ladia was ready for some action and this last hour had been sort of action-free.

I looked at Rey, "Well, we sort of figured that four hours was enough time."

"Time for what?"

"Ella is being held at Handlon. It's only half a mile from Ionia. They're going to expect us to be there immediately afterward, before, or at the same time. They won't expect us to lie low for four hours, then hit it."

"So, we lie low for a few more hours? Where do we do that?"

Symone made her way through the Aft door into the private area. "Welcome to the bottom of the Grand River."

"We're sleeping with the fishies." Ladia confirmed.

"Nope. No fish. They dredged it, so it's deeper. But we're barely underwater. It's only like fifteen meters down. Just enough water to hide us, I hope," Symone grabbed a bottle of water from the fridge and handed us each one.

"Damn. From an American war prison camp to drinking fancy water in a pricey submarine." Ladia leaned back and relaxed a bit.

Rey sat down, "Before we move on, do we need anything- medication, anything?"

I took a drink, "the lab is well stocked. I would ask Ladia about the Medkits."

As Ladia detailed what we needed, I excused myself and moved into the back bathroom. The room had two additional toilets and a suite of showers. Behind the big basin-like sink was a long mirror that stretched across the wall, from one side to the other completely. The lights turned on as I walked in, turning on the water to wipe my face.

This was the first time I'd been alone since what had happened outside. Did I just have some weird premonition that alerted me? It seemed so real. I really felt like I had been blown to shreds. And then, bam, a second later, I was back at the beginning, in the Fearless, right before we stopped. I'd asked myself all the reasonable questions. So I started with UNreasonable.

Was it some sort of time bomb? Do things like that exist? I had honestly never seen anything like that bomb before. It didn't look like American tech.

So where did it come from?

***

We showered and changed, getting ready for lunch. I probably should explain a little about my leadership style. As I mentioned, I'm not super high protocol.

Protocol gets in the way.

I grew up on horror movies. You'll notice that, eventually. Scream. Scream 2. The next one after that. Final Destination. That had some sequels, too. Ghost stories, monster stories, etc. If you ever need life advice, just put on a horror film and do the opposite. It's sort of genius.

You might have noticed my Poltergeist reference earlier. It was one of my favorites. When the uppity ghosts kidnapped Carole-anne, an adorable blonde child, and stashed her in the matrix of the television (I didn't write it) the tiny medium spiritualist advised her not to "go into the light."

Until she had to go into the light. It's sloppy writing, but it makes sense. In the movie.

And, yes, they're silly and sometimes pointless and overwritten, but I've learned one big thing from horror movies.

Keeping things to yourself just makes the movie last longer. How many movies have you seen that would have been over in ten minutes if the main characters had just come clean and told each other what they knew?

I am uninterested in that performative shit.

"Ok, guys, for lunch today, I want to introduce a new ongoing game. You guys tell me anything at all that you think is going on that feels weird or unusual and I tell you my weird stuff. How does that sound? Nothing's too weird."

Ladia was used to my idiosyncrasies and I wasn't much worried about her. The other two, however, this is where they get to decide if I'm too nuts to lead.

"I like it." Rey filled a bowl with the mushroom barley stew Symone had put together for lunch. He slid his chair and started eating. I was more concerned about his response than the women. He seemed very "by the book" to me.

Symone seemned much more casual, I guess.

And she was.

"I love it." She grabbed her bowl and filled it. "In fact, I dig it so much, I'm going to go first." She stuffed a spoonful into her mouth and grabbed a remote from the center of the table. She pointed it at the wall and it filled with an underwater visual.

Ladia looked over, "Nice. Way better than a window. Less wet than a hole."

"Windows don't do this." Symone pushed a button and the view zoomed in. There was water around us. And it was shifting and moving.

"All right, what are those?" Rey pointed to the thousands of tiny fish that were swimming around the ship.

"Liar. I thought you said there were no fish in this lake." Ladia seemed to be enjoying her first real meal since we'd entered ionia.

I squinted. These were unlike any fish I'd seen. Symone zoomed in further. They had rows of metallic looking teeth that vibrated and rotated, like a circular saw. "What the fuck."

Symone put the remote down and continued eating, "There shouldn't be any fish at all. But certainly not these. I don't know what these are."

I walked over to the wall monitor. "Should we be concerned that they're actually leaving scratches on the hull?"

"I don't know. I mean, I'm just concerned they're there, honestly. They don't match any species in the database." Symone shrugged. "None."

"Well." Rey got up to get a better look, too. "That is certainly weird.

Ladia asked, "Do we worry about these guys right now? Or will we be gone before they're a problem?"

"Oh, they aren't a big problem right now. Just weird and worth watching. And, that's all I have." Symone sat back down.

Rey nodded, "ok, here's mine. It's not really that weird. But do any of you think that was too easy?"

Ladia furrowed her brow, "What was? The breakout?"

"Yes. I was expecting a lot more resistance. It was incredibly smooth."

I looked over at Rey. He might have a point. Or he might have been giving the jailers too much credit. "Ok. It did go very easily. A lot could have gone wrong and it didn't. In a way, it felt familiar."

"Exactly."

"You planned better than you thought." Ladia was there. She had an opinion of her own. "But, realistically, those people were idiots. I mean, you had a phone, I snuck out of my cell almost every night, and don't get me started on camera blindspots."

Rey seemed to weigh that in his head, "ok. I'll take that. It wasn't easy. They were just morons."

Ladia shrugged and continued eating, "Sometimes the enemy is just dumb as paper towels."

Symone raised her glass, "To more stupid enemies."

I grabbed my glass. I would toast to that.

"Mine's a little bigger. And I think I need you to promise me that you won't toss me out the hatch with the razorfish."

I had everyone's attention now. "I think I died back there."

Ladia stopped. "Like, psychologically?"

"It felt like a temporary glitch." Symone stopped the ship and we ran out. I tried to remove the bomb and it exploded. I was cut in half. A second later, time had reversed and I stopped the ship. I recognized the bomb. I detonated it remotely."

I looked over at Rey. He looked concerned but not the kind where he wanted me removed from command. "And this felt real to you?"

"Real. As. Fuck." I realized I'd been holding my breath. "Has anyone experienced any sort of time dilations or reversals or anything?"

I looked around the room. They were all shaking their heads.

Symone thought for a second, "ok, so what you're saying is that time went by a certain way, reversed, and then it went a different way?"

"Yes. The second loop I didn't die."

"So, it was changeable. The timeline?"

"Yes. Apparently. I remembered and I changed it."

"And that bomb ITSELF was weird." Ladia offered up.

Symone was trying to put it all together, "Right. That goes in the 'weird things trying to hurt us' category. This time jump goes into the other bucket- 'weird things trying to help us.' - Like in that movie."

"Unless it was a hallucination." I confessed that this had been nagging at me. "Wait- what movie?"

"Oh, I remember. It was a movie with Tom Cruise. You probably didn't see it because there wasn't enough blood." Ladia suggested.

Symone seemingly had, "he is fighting alien creatures and every time he dies, he sort of snaps back. Alive. to a point before he died."

"Holy shit." I made a point to look for the movie in the archives. "That's exactly what happened."

Rey finished eating and took his bowl to the dishwasher. "Ok, so we should be prepared for devices, like that bomb, that either create unstable, what...? temporal conditions or..."

I finished for him. "Or create hallucinations. And we should look fot that movie"

The ship moved slightly. It wasn't much, but it was noticeable. I looked over and saw, on the wall monitor, one of the fish was larger - nearly five centimeters long.

"That didn't cause that, did it?"

Symone got up and moved toward the door. "I don't care. It's time to get out of here."

***

It was dark when we crawled out of the water. The night seemed quiet, and it was almost easy to forget where we were going and what we were about to do. Rey, Ladia, and I changed into the blue black suits of the COs of Handlon. Ionia was a brute force operation, blowing out the wall and scooping us up.

So this Jailbreak would be the opposite. We would dress as guards, sneak in, liberate our one resident, and get back to the Fearless as fast as we could.

"You look like shit, cowboy," Ladia did not appreciate the ensemble.

"Don't make me and the English guy arrest you, Canuck." I looked over at Rey. I could tell he was uncomfortable in that foreign uniform. He pressed the little knob at his neck and the mask went up. Ladia and I did the same.

Best if no one saw our faces.

We stood in the Triage area, near the open doorway to the NavPod. Symone called out. "Ok. two minutes. I'm hiding behind the water tower thing and you guys use your fake passes and get in. I'll keep the motor running, but if you're longer than a few minutes they may find me."

I eyed my watch and set a silent timer.

"Got it." Looking up at the monitor wall one more time, I committed the layout of Handlon to memory. I could see Ella Campbell's cell, located conveniently near the facility's main entrance.

I switched on the voice changer and yelled out, gruffly, in a man's voice, "ok, let's move this out."

We poured out the Starboard Triage bay and moved as mechanically as possible to the front gate. The passes opened the gates easily and even allowed access to the door. The guard at the front door began bitching at me until I pulled rank. He shut up quickly and let us through.

We followed the lines on the floor to the cell block where we had hoped to find Ella. And that's when my heart sank.

Her cell was empty. And so were the two adjacent to it. I looked at Ladia and she shrugged. I pointed to Rey to stand by the door and I approached the guard closest to me. I pulled the gun from the holster on my CO uniform and shoved it in his face.

"15 seconds to tell me where these prisoners are."

Ladia counted down without pausing, "15, 13, 9, 7, 6…"

"Wait, wait. Electric Room, Electric room."

I hit him upside the head with the butt of a gun and he went down, quickly. Ladia looked over at the next nearest guard and her newly male voice boomed out, sounding like some kind of weird warning, "I'm not a math person."

I followed the eyes of one of the guards to the right corridor and saw the stenciled lightning bolt on the door.

Rey pressed his credentials against the lock and I pushed the door in.

Two guards stood in the center of the room. Against one wall, three women were hanging by ropes in their underwear. The shorter of the two guards had a thick Salvador Dali mustache with a crew cut. He looked us over.

"Who the fuck are you?"

As my eyes adjusted to the light, I could see that Ella was the leftmost woman hanging near the wall.

"Hey, guys. I meant to meet you." She tried to wave.

""I said who the fuck are you?" Salvador Dali twitched and fell as Rey tased him. The other CO raised his hands as if to surrender.

Ladia shook her head and started untying the women, starting with Ella. "Are you doing ok?"

Ella was surprisingly cheerful, "We were about to be sexually assaulted."

I tased the taller guy who squirmed and seemed reluctant to pass out, "No shit."

"I mean, I have my doubts about how that would have gone." The other two women seemed equally unphased. They dropped to the floor as Ladia released them.

"Ok, let's strip Dali and Picasso here. Ladies, you are all being promoted to CO. Congratulations."

"I told you all your hard work would pay off." Ella helped the other two. They shared pieces of uniform. I tased the taller guard again. At one point, it was punitive. I had never learned how many consecutive times you could tase someone. In the back of my head I remembered a number. I think it was something like six.

It looked like we'd be walking out of here with a couple more people than we'd thought.

Suddenly, there was a pop and the room went dark. I dove behind a panel I remembered next to me and waited for my eyes to accustom themselves to the black. Two shots rang out, from one of the COs guns, no doubt. A second later, a red safety light went on and I could see Dali holding Ella. Her hands were covered in what looked like mud and he held a gun to her head. I looked down at the taller one who appeared to have been shot in the face.

"Did he shoot his friend in the face?"

Rey seemed confused, "I think killing his friend was supposed to scare us?"

"It was a fucking accident, ok?" Dali tottered behind Ella.

Ladia spoke to Ella, "I'm scared. How about you?"

"I'm mostly cold and want to put some clothes on," The other two women nodded. She turned her head to him, "You don't think the moment has passed?"

I kept the little red dot from my gun trained on Dali's forehead. "I'm not an expert, but I think this sexual assault is going poorly, mustache."

Ladia nodded. "Yeah, a smart guard would give it up."

"Shut the fuck up. All of you. I'm walking out of here."

Ella rolled her eyes and quickly pulled her arms out, simultaneously. It was hard to understand what she was doing, it all happened so quickly. Dali fell behind her as an explosion of tiny objects shot out onto the floor. He started to cry rolling around. I saw now that the mud on her hands was blood, rendered black by the red lights. She had grabbed two handfuls of glass from the blown out light bulbs and used them, just now, to slice all of his fingers off.

Every one of them.

Ladia kicked Dali on the floor and made her way to Ella, finishing the job of dressing the three women.

"That was gross. I missed you, peanut." Ladia hugged Ella who then dropped to the ground, looking around. For the second time that day, my heart sank.

"El, are you trying to find all the fingers?"

"I'm probably the only surgeon in 200 kilometers who can reattach them."

I looked at my watch. We were there for five minutes.

"Fuck." I pulled out the tranq and shot the twitching man on the ground, imagining how I could take an unconscious guard past the front gate. I looked around the room and saw an equipment box not much bigger than a picnic cooler.

As I stepped over, I found myself praying it had wheels.

4 - Hidden

Rey was moving us as far away from Handlon as we could get while Symone sat with us on the front couch in the Triage Bay, kicking the equipment trunk.

"Tell me he's fucking bleeding to death in there."

'Nope." Ella had bandaged his hands up quickly before we left, bagging all ten of his errant fingers. She fished through the medical storage area preparing for the surgery. "But it is not comfortable."

Her fellow inmates were changing out of the clumsy guard outfits into some clean clothes, taking turns in the forward bathroom. The first of them, Rosette, a pretty redhead with big eyes and a chiseled looking six pack stepped out of the bathroom. "Oh, my god. I smell so good. Seriously, I want to marry your shower."

The other one, Gillian, a dark-haired light skinned black woman with a wide smile, put her hand in mine. "I can't thank you enough for getting us the hell out of there."

"And the timing was impeccable," Rosette offered up. "Chef's kiss."

"We just can't pass up a three for one deal." Lydia moved the trunk to the middle of the room, kicking it to set it in place.

I shook my head. "Can anyone tell me why we shouldn't toss this little package out right now?"

"Hey, fuck you." Dali spat out from inside.

"That's so cute. He's barking," Gillian pulled her long hair up into a tight bun and shoved it under a hat.

"I'm sorry, guys. I took an oath. I can reattach his fingers and I should." Ella assembled everything she'd need.

"There's a clean room right off the Lab. It's like two and a half meters by one and a half but we can do it there. I'll assist. Then we'll drop fingerbang, here, off over the border." Ladia looked at me and shrugged.

I sighed. "You three were the only trans women in Handlon?"

"Affirmative, Colonel. They had us in contiguous cells. " Ella didn't look up.

"But once we regroup, you can drop us back off, too. We can get the rest of our people out."

I pressed my hand against the inner storage space and the images of the weapons inside showed on the monitor wall. "Just let us know what you need."

Rosette looked impressed. She looked at Gillan. "We'll take one of everything."

***

We dropped the women off, against my better judgment, about five miles away from Handlon. They seemed to have a plan and I respected that. We still had a few things to accomplish as well. Symone rested while Rey and I drove the hour and a half toward the Hidden Valley mobile home encampment. Picking up the last member of our team would give Ella and Ladia the time to reattach dickhead's fingers.

I made a mental note to determine his real name one day. I leaned back in the co-pilot seat. I still hadn't had the chance to drive this thing.

"So, there's a story about why our guy...."

"Filo"

"Yes, Filo. Why he is in a mobile home in Michigan, waiting for us."

"There actually is." Rey squinted a little. Part of the screen in front of was in infrared mode so we could drive at night without any lights. It really wasn't easy on the eyes.

"He actually defected a few years ago. To me. But he was working on something with his cousin here over the border, when the war broke out. Now that he's finished it, though, he wants to demonstrate it for us."

"And what is it?"

"I have no idea. He wanted to tell us in person. He's squirrely like that."

"Well, he'll get his chance in about twenty eight minutes, it looks like."

"Hidden Valley is a center for the American Resistance."

"No shit, where they make the ranch?"

"Actually, I'm not sure if they are the same. But let's say so."

"Ranch and resistance."

Rey smiled. It wasn't yet common enough for me not to find amusing. "And what is Filo like?"

"Oh, you'll like him. He's very smart. He's very technology forward."

"Well, that doesn't suck."

"If we do keep encountering 'weird' types of technology out here he will be useful, for sure."

"And that's our six?"

Rey nodded, "That is our six. I like your doctor friend. She's got energy. Plus a moral code. That's a good combination."

"She won't let us down, ever. I'm sure of it."

"At some point, I hope you will be just as sure of the three of us," He nodded his head to Symone.

This was my chance to pull us together as one team. When you lead people, you look for those chances. You can't invent them, you have to respond to them.

"Brother. I think that happened at some point during our second successful prison break."

Rey smiled wide. Still amusing. "Whatever Filo has for us, it's big. I've worked with him a lot. He doesn't get excited by a lot of tech."

"Anything else I should know? You know, in the spirit of our transparency?"

"Well. Some people are people people and some people are technology people…"

"And he's the second one?"

"In all possible ways."

"Got it." I pressed the comlink to the clean room. "Hey, Nurseface, how's it going in there?"

Ladia's voice rang out in the NavPod, "Commander Mittens is unconscious and quiet, so it's actually kind of relaxing in here. Over"

"How much longer do you need?"

"One sec. Ok, Dr. Badass is mercilessly mocking the patient by holding up three fingers. It looks like we need three more hours."

"Ok. take your time, you two. Bond. Keep that fucker medicated."

"Roger, Sir."

I turned to Rey. "Looks like it's just you and me in Ranchtown."

***

Resistance members pulled a silver tarp over the Fearless. Standing outside of it again I was reminded how huge it was. It was as if people stapled two massive school buses together side by side. The tank treads came up past my waist.

I pointed to a small device at the top of the tarp. "So what is that?"

Rey stepped over and peered up. The dark was pervasive. "Oh, that's a disperser. It stops the ship from radiating heat. That way it won't show up on sensor passes from planes, etc."

"It doesn't look familiar."

"You were in that camp for a while." He looked down. He wasn't wrong. "This is Myles and this is Jamie. They are American Resistance."

"Good to meet you." I held out my hand.

Myles grabbed it. "Nice to meet you Colonel. I know it's late. But you're going to want to see this."

The two men walked sharply toward a larger trailer, covered in graffiti. If I needed to hide a technological secret, I would choose this trailer.

I recognized Filo right away from his file. He was young. No older than twenty five. There was a shock of black hair on top of his head, shaved around the sides, over a heavy brow and pouting lips. He was heavily tattooed and sported a big ring earring in each ear. He looked more like a graffiti artist than a soldier. So when he turned to me and saluted, I was initially taken aback.

"Colonel."

I leaned in to shake his hand. "You can put that away, soldier. I'm not big on protocol. Good to meet you."

"I've heard a lot about you." His accent was American. According to his file, he had defected to Canada before the start of the war. I'd heard a lot about him, too.

"So, you're in it the hard way, huh?"

He turned to the man next to him - I was betting it was his brother - and laughed. "I like how you put that."

"Is this your brother?" I nodded to the man next to him.

"Yep. This is Manny. But these are all my brothers." He motioned to Myles and Jamie and the two women in the back of the trailer. "A couple of sisters back there." they waved.

"I get that. I hear you have something amazing to show me."

They all smiled widely, "I do."

I turned to Rey, "Do you already know?"

He shrugged, "I'm in the dark as much as you are."

Filo started. "Ok, so, i've been sneaking back and forth over the border for the last year with the guys. And we've been noticing some weird shit. Strange technology, even some strange animals. Just weird."

I looked at Rey, "That tracks. We've seen some of that, too. You saw a lot of it?"

"A lot. And there seems to be more all the time. I've been categorizing it and tracking it."

"And using it?" I leaned in.

"That's just it. I can use it. But first I wanted to know where it came from."

"I'd be interested to know that, too," Rey countered.

"Well, After a lot of examination and talking to random Americans and reading various fucked up websites, I think I now know where.

Not from this planet. And not from this time.

That was an alarm. "Wait, from a different planet and time?"

"Yes." He pressed a button and a series of swirling rings showed up in 3D. "This is the list of elements found on earth." he pressed another button and the rings filled in more. "This is the list of elements that probably exist elsewhere" and hit a third. The rings filled the screen. "And this is the composition of the found technology."

"And you ran every test?"

"I did." He reached into a drawer and pulled out a small gun-like shape. "I tested this exhaustively."

"Ok. a gun?" It looked odd. Different than any gun I'd seen.

"Because this." he pointed the gun upward and a beam of light flashed from it, opening a small hole in the roof. I noticed now that the roof was peppered with these small holes.

Rey was impressed, too, "Damn. And what did you learn?"

"At first, nothing. But then we discovered this." He pulled out a small device the size of a phone with a screen on it. "It took us a while, but we figured it out. It's an accelerator mass spectrometer. Or part of it is."

"That I know. So you can use that to figure out what these are made of?"

File seemed excited I wasn't a complete idiot. "Right. But I can also find trace elements that are only there in tiny tiny amounts. Like P-244"

My eyes opened. I looked to Rey, "Plutonium 244 is possibly a primordial element. It has a half-life of over 81 million years. And detecting it is hard."

"We learned…" Filo picked up the spectrometer and Manny lifted the ray gun. They moved them together until it let out a beep. "…This" He showed me the tiny screen.

"No fucking way. This thing is from about eight hundred years in the future and a different planet. " I peered at it.

"A temporal anomaly." Filo's face was completely lit up.

Rey gingerly reached for the gun, "How is this even possible?"

"Is this what you wanted to show us? It's pretty impressive."

Filo and Manny laughed. "No, that's just the backstory. I have a bunch of these guns for the ship, but over here is my real gift for her."

We moved over a few feet to a box-like structure with a towel thrown over it hastily. Rey put his hand on Filo's shoulder paternally. He looked about as proud as it was possible to be. Filo put his hand over Rey's. I realized I didn't know how long it had been since they'd seen each other. I tried to take in the environment. The mess surrounding me in this trailer was starting to look more intentional - more dramatic. Filo pulled off the towel.

"Ta da. I call it the aggregator." Filo waved his hands at a clean chrome box with a touch screen panel in the front and a door that went from one side to the other. It looked shockingly familiar.

"A microwave?" I looked at it. It sure was pretty.

"Not quite." Filo looked over at Manny. He continued, "ok, so those guns don't have a power source. We opened them up and saw that they were sort of aggregating the energy around them and converting it to solid light. They basically suck energy from the universe and use it to make something. So we figured out how to do that."

"Just not as a weapon." Filo smiled.

"It's 3 am, what do you want?"

A nap. This was me being honest. "I've been in prison. I would kill you all for a Nanaimo Bar. "

Filo thought for a second, then typed onto the screen. "Got it."

There was a slight ding and he nodded at me. I opened the door and pulled out a perfectly set Nanaimo bar. I glanced at Rey.

"Is that safe? To eat?" Rey sounded particularly British when he was being cautious.

"In every way." Filo motioned to me and I took a bite. It seemed like everyone held their breath.

"This is great." I slid the rest into my mouth. The custard was just right and the chocolate ganache on top melted as you pressed your tongue down on it.

Rey whispered, "Aggregator?"

Filo nodded, "Very first one. For the fearless. Anything you want."

The room erupted in cheers.

Suddenly, my comm went off. It was Ella.

"Colonel, We're done. That went faster than I thought. We'll get cleaned up and join you."

"It's all good, El. We're coming back to the Fearless. Just figure out what you want to eat. Both of you." I looked around the room where everyone was still celebrating and I thought about the little chocolate bomb from my youth I had just eaten.

"Oh. And make it weird."

***

Jamie and Mannie joined us on the ship to install the aggregator. We placed it up near the stove. It was bizarre to me that there was no plug and it wasn't tied into any power at all.

Ladia took a bit out of an ice cream cone and dressed down Filo. "Aren't any of the laws of thermodynamics sacred to you?"

Filo laughed. "How is that?"

"This is literally the greatest thing I've ever eaten. I used to eat these in grade school. How is this thing even possible?"

"It's crazy, isn't it? Can I put the rest of my stuff in the lab?"

I looked over at Ladia. "Ice cream girl, you want to show the guys the lab? And show them where to put the weapons"

She looked at Filo, "It's LIEUTENANT Ice Cream girl. C'mon, Ice cream man, let's get your shit planted." She moved off with Filo and his friends.

I stepped into the bathroom and ran some water over my face. As soon as we were on our way, we'd have our complete crew. Then it was time to get to work.

A series of shots rang out, dragging me out of my reverie. I shot out of the bathroom with my gun in my hand. Rey and Ella were to my right, by the back couch. I dove toward the center corridor and then through the door into the lab, I saw Ladia on the floor, covered in blood. Filo, Manny, and Jamie were in a pile right next to her, dead.

I took a breath and lifted my gun. I turned to the left and saw the guard standing there, a string in his teeth, wrapped around the trigger for a rifle. He pulled his head back and I felt the bullet collapse my forehead and tear through my brain. I spun and hit the ground hard.

***

Rey opened the Triage Bay doors and we stepped on, carrying the aggregator. Memories hit me like a wave. This time it was faster.

The guard.

I motioned to Rey and moved to the Nav Pod door. From there, we could enter the Lab. The lab door swung open and it was empty.

Rey and I moved to the doorway to the clean room and held our guns up.

The door hissed open and the guard stood there, rifle hanging from under his arm. He looked me in the eye.

"Oh, fuck."

And I slammed my gun into his head. He fell backward.

I pulled the rifle away and Rey and I dragged him into the center corridor and then to the triage bay.

Filo was standing there with his gun trained on him. "Who is this guy?"

"It's ok. He should have been unconscious. I had a... I had a feeling he wasn't."

Filo walked over to him. "He's American? A prison guard?"

"Yes. Ella was reattaching the fingers she cut off him."

Manny whistled, "You guys know how to party."

Ladia and Ella stepped into Triage. "He was tied up. And he should be out for hours still." Ladia looked confused.

Filo looked over, lowering his gun. "Well. The bad news is... I've seen these on guards." He pulled a device off the back of the guard's neck. "It's a drainer. It prevents them from being drugged."

Ella shook her head. "So, wait. He was awake for hours,while I reattached his fingers just so he could play possum and what, kill us?"

I rubbed my forehead. That was exactly what he did. I looked at Rey, "It happened again."

Filo glanced back and forth at us. "What happened?"

"She experienced some sort of time dilation or something. Time seemed to reverse."

"And I went from being dead to realizing what I needed to do. In the original timeline, he killed everyone."

Ella breathed in and out quickly. "Look, it wasn't your fault." I said, holding her arms.

"How did he sit through an operation awake without making a sound?" Ella was terrified.

"That's it, you." Ladia grabbed him and stuffed him back into the gear trunk. "Back to your convenient carrying case."

Ella whispered to me, "You're having hallucinations?"

"That's just it, I don't think they are."

Rey perked up, "If they are hallucinations, they are deadly accurate."

Filo looked down, "Damn."

I surveyed the room. "We've sort of established this policy of being open about weird stuff. If you've got something weird to share, please, bombs away."

Filo raised his hand. "I don't think they're hallucinations, either." He was staring at the device in his hand. Rey looked confused and moved over to him, lifting the device.

"'I second that."

"What does that say?" I felt the room spin around me a bit. Filo held it up.

"It's you. You're a temporal anomaly, too."

5 - RK

"So, wait, I'm from 800 years in the future?" I sat on the table in the lab while Filo fiddled with the accelerator. Ella was taking my vital signs and Rey...

Rey was just worrying.

Ladia and Symone were in the Triage Bay watching over the Trunk where the prison guard was stuffed. And I didn't FEEL like I was from 800 years in the future.

"No. But none of this makes any sense. It says you are from about eighteen months in the past."

"What the fuck? What does that mean?"

Filo shook his head, "I don't really know."

"Does this mean I'm compromised?"

Rey shot a quick look at Filo, waiting for his response.

"I really don't don't think so. Your readings are very different from the American tech stuff. In fact, the opposite."

"What could cause this?" Rey looked at me.

"Well, a few things. If she was in some kind of temporal suspension for about eighteen months."

"How would that work?" Ella was curious, as well. "Would there be physical signs?"

"Well, yeah. These. But I don't know." Filo looked into my eyes, "Do you have any lost time?"

"No. But if I did, would I know?"

Ella started the math in her head, "ok, the crash was about eighteen months ago, right?"

"I think so." If I tried to work it out in my head, I realized that I may have been unconscious for longer than I thought. Ladia would know.

Rey shook his head, as if trying to disperse the entire range of recent events. We'd been moving for the entire day now and he could tell everyone was tired. "She's safe, not in any danger. We should pick this back up tomorrow."

I let out a sigh. In theory, I agreed with that. "One last thing. Before we crash, I want to know what the guy in the trunk knows." I looked around the room. "All of it."

***

I stared down at the trunk. It would probably take us about fifteen minutes in the Triage bay to get him out of the trunk and cleaned up. It was possible all we were going to get out of him was a stream of expletives. I didn't care.

We had open questions.

"Hey, Mittens." I kicked the trunk. I could hear his breathing, heavy. It seemed like he was keeping to himself now. I could already tell this wouldn't yield much.

Ladia and Rey were holding guns at the trunk, waiting for Filo to pop open the top. The room seemed to hang there, pregnant, waiting on my word.

"All right. Let's pop this top."

Filo opened the trunk. Right away, I could tell something was different. He was curled up and his breathing was heavy and slow.

Ella scrunched her face up. "Been a bad day for him."

"Well, he's making it a bad day for me." I sighed and kicked the trunk again. At this point, I think everyone just wanted to go to bed. "Hey, fingergloves. Up we go."

Faster that I would have thought possible, his head spun around and his face did something I'd never seen before. Right down the center, it seemed to split open, horizontally, revealing a blood red maw in the center, ringed with tiny metal-looking teeth. He growled and spat as we all jumped up and backed away.

Still breathing heavily, his head lifted up from the trunk straight up and spun again in the other direction. It was as if his face was able to move 360 degrees around his skull. His body, seemingly longer and more emaciated than when he went into the trunk, snapped and unfolded, pulling him from the trunk in jerky movements, nearly too fast to see.

"What the fuck." Ladia was the first one to fire. She put two bullets right through his neck. His head fell backward then snapped back up as he reached for her. Rey and I shot him in the head.

It did nothing.

We kept firing. He moved toward Ella in jerky motions, savagely and almost too fast to see. She reached out and grabbed at his hand, pulling hard. Three of the fingers she had worked so hard to reattach came off, dropping to the floor as he stopped, just for a second.

I palmed the storage area and pulled out a crovel. It was black and sleek and as long as my arm. One flip and it opened up so I could slide it cleanly through the guard's neck, severing his head.

His body fell to the floor in a panic, spinning, spitting blood all over.

His head dropped and rolled into the far corner of the bay, near the sink. The front opened wider and two blood red tentacles slithered out over its teeth, dragging the head under the sink, out of view.

Filo emptied his gun under the sink. "Holy shit."

The thing's body was flailing, crawling toward the sink, as though it could feel where its head was. I lifted the crovel and stabbed it through the ribcage, impaling it in place, digging into the black rubber floor. It spit a fountain of dark red from the neck, painting Symone with decaying bloody mud. It twitched and fell quiet.

I could hear the wheeze of the head, still breathing, tucked away in the space under the sink.

"It's still alive," Rey whispered to me. I shrugged with wide eyes. Yes. It was clearly still alive.

Ella came in through the Nav pod door. I hadn't seen her leave. She stomped over to the sink and lifted a rifle in one hand. With the other she emptied a jar into the space where the head had hidden. It screeched and crawled out like a spider, tentacles dragging the bulk of the skull across the floor. She fired again and again, destroying the brain, the last shot sending it toward the far wall where it laid inert.

We all stood there for a minute. Symone let out a scream. I turned to her as she took a deep breath.

She looked around the room at us. "I meant to do that earlier."

***

Filo's brother came back out to help us clean out the triage space. None of us could sleep until all the bloody mess was gone. He had never seen anything like this. No one in the resistance had. Filo himself was fascinated that Ella was able to synthesize hydrofluoric acid in the aggregator. He had been imagining it a sort of food synthesizer. The two of them, along with Symone, were synthesizing the things we'd need to clean all this.

Already the team was building on each other.

I slipped the remains of Dali's head into a metal bucket. "This seems a little severe for a post-surgical complication."

Rey was working on cutting the body up with a microsaw and bagging it. "I'm guessing that these are all biowaste. A hazard."

"Yeah, I don't want anyone touching any of these or even breathing anything in until we figure out what happened."

Manny nodded. "You guys really do party hard, though."

Ladia laughed, "This was the worst party I've ever seen."

I stood up and put a rubber top on the bucket. "So, none of you have ever seen anything like this before?"

Manny shook his head. "Never. You say he was just a guard at Handlon?"

Rey was taping the bags together. "Yes."

"And that thing that used to be on his neck?"

I shook my head, "Your brother said it was a disperser - no, a drainer, or something, used to eliminate drugs and toxins from the system."

Ladia scrunched up her face. "We took it off and then he turned into this?"

I was following, "Do you think he had a chemical in his body making him into this and it only started kicking in when we removed that thing?"

Rey looked up at us, "That would be a twisted thing to do. Infect the guard with something like this."

It hit me. Yes. It would be. "Hey, can you guys finish up? I want to take another look at that drainer."

***

Filo, Ella, and I squinted down at the device on the lab table. It was a disk, maybe 4 centimeters in diameter.

"So what do you think?" I asked.

Filo moved the tweezers to one side. "You see that nub?"

"I do."

"I think that's the receiver. I think you're right. it can be deactivated remotely."

Ella whistled, "So you infect your guards with some monster disease, put one of these on it to keep the disease at bay and then turn it off remotely whenever you feel like it…"

"And create a monster." I was both amazed and disgusted at the same time.

Filo looked at Ella, "And you were in this men's prison just because you're trans?"

She nodded.

"They didn't attach anything to you? You ok?" he put his hand on hers.

She put her other hand on top of his and smiled. "Trust me, I'm better than him."

"Nice move with the acid, too."

I rolled my eyes at this little mutual admiration society. "And you had no idea, in Handlon, that they did any of this?"

"No. I never saw it. But if he's right, it's an infection."

"We're already at pathogen alert." My skin was still crawling, though.

"It makes sense, I guess, if you think like a fucking insane person." Filo seemed to be running scenarios in his head. "Let's say you have a riot. You need to activate a group of COs to end it. Then you do what?"

"You clean it all up." I finished, "So no one knows."

"Do you think the guards know?" Ella looked horrified

"I bet they don't. Look at how small all this is. But they have to know that something is up. I actually don't think you could even get drunk with one of these on."

"Ok, I'm done with episode one of 'the horrors of war.' I say we get some rest. I'll take the first watch in the Nav Pod. You guys all get cleaned up and get to bed."

***

It was dark and quiet in the Nav Pod as I slid over and lifted my legs onto the leather seat next to me. I figured I could use this time to try and find my missing eighteen months. The crash was, in my mind, about that time. A year and a half ago.

I tried to set the Ting down lightly, until I found out it was just a big bomb. Then the job was to keep it away from populated areas. We were just over the border when it started to come apart. I lost the back of the plane, along with any control I might have pretended to have. I closed my eyes and saw Herman sucked out of a hoe in the side as he tried to rescue Ladia in the cockpit.

In a split second, he was gone. All the time we'd spent together, everything he had done, everything he was, gone.

The plane set down hard. I couldn't move. The cockpit was on fire. I closed my eyes.

I woke up in Ionia, strapped to a table, healing. There was my first chunk of lost time. How long did it take me to heal? I don't remember the infirmary at all. Ladia and I never talked about how long it had taken us to get back on our feet after the crash.

How long had it been since we set down?

I felt detached from the answer. I guess, sitting in a prison cell, it didn't much matter. Did they put my body in some kind of cellular suspension? Why just me and not Ladia?

None of it made any sense.

I called up the external cameras. It looked quiet out there. Everybody seemed tucked into their mobile homes. It was still a few more hours until morning. The motion sensors buzzed and I pressed the button to shift the cameras. I saw a quick flutter of movement behind Filo's brother's Mobile home. It was almost imperceptible, like a rag in the wind. I zoomed in the camera.

Then, it fluttered again.

I looked more closely. It was only a couple of rats.

I breathed out, realizing that I had been holding my breath.

I watched the rats through the cameras. I caught a glint off of one of them. They both dove under the mobile home. I searched some more, but they were gone.

I pressed the screen to rewind the recording. I wound it back to the glint I had seen and stopped it. I zoomed in. There, on the back of one of the rats was a 4 centimeter long metal disk.

A drainer.

***

By sunrise I'd managed to learn enough about the sensor equipment to track and list all the small animals in the mobile park.

"Two thousand, three hundred and twelve," Ray intoned in his classier-than-though accent.

"It sounds better when you say it." I put the breakdown on the screen. Only forty-two of those were cats or dogs. The rest were rats.

Filo looked at the two of us. "Is that a normal number of rats digging around under a mobile home park? Because that's nasty. "

I shook my head. "I really don't know. But of the two thousand plus rats, only about sixty have devices on them."

"Devices that could be triggered remotely at any time." Rey finished.

"Yep. I set the sensors to go off with any morphological changes to any of those. I already contacted your brother and he's getting all these people ready to bug out. But the last thing i wanted to do was to go out in the pitch black and fuck with rat monsters."

"Yeah. Yuck." Filo shook his head.

"It's like a dirty bomb, just waiting to go off." Rey was pacing now.

"I didn't want to wake you two up, but that's the deal. Walk through this with me."

Rey sat down. "Ok." I know he was used to a lot more stringent protocol. I was really impressed with how flexible he was flying my way, sort of by the seat of our pants.

I started, "My assumption is that those sixty rats are infected with this Zombie disease."

"Right. Why else attach a drainer to them? They are little secret murder agents." Filo had already made the leap I made last night. This monster disease also affects rats, turning them into....What?

Rey looked up, imagining, "So we kill them, but we run the risk of damaging one of the units."

"Ok, that's bad day scenario one. We try to kill them, one or two get triggered, infect the rest, rat monsters everywhere." I mentally checked that off in my mind.

Filo picked up, "Bad Day scenario two, they set some, OR ALL OF THEM, off remotely, and we have sixty of those things, they infect the rest, rat monsters everywhere."

Rey chimed in, "Bad Day scenario three. One of these sixty rats, crawling around, accidentally scrapes one of these devices off, they go monster, infect the rest, rat monsters everywhere."

"Good day scenario, devices were put on these rats unmonitored and no one ever triggers them, maybe people forget they're there." My voice raised hopefully.

"No. this place is burned." Filo ran his hands through his hair.

"What sucks is that only Bad Day Scenario number one lets us have a reasonable chance of containing it." I didn't want to believe that, but it was true. "Fiko, is there anything you can do to prevent these things from going off until we kill the rats?"

"I don't know. Give me a little time to research?"

"You have an hour. I'll signal Manny. Then begins Operation Ratkiller."

Filo stepped through the door to the lab. Rey turned to me, "Is that what we're calling this?"

"It just came to me. You don't like it?"

"No, it's good. It's on the nose."

"I have no subtlety. We need to get everyone up and briefed. This is going to suck,"

An alarm shot through the ship. Looking down at the sensor panel I saw three red dots. Three of the rats had been activated. That was too many to have been an accident.

"Bad day scenario 2."

Rey grabbed his gun, "That was my least favorite."

Ladia was the first one through the door, "What the hell?"

"Get everyone into Triage Bay with weapons. We're under attack."

"Roger." she dove back through the triage door. Rey and I followed.

Within a second or two, all six of us were at the center storage door, grabbing weapons.

"I hate this, but I've been tracking rats all night with those little devices on them. I found 60. There are hundreds more rats, all timebombs, waiting to go off. Three of them just turned."

"So we're fighting rat monsters?" Ella called out.

"And anything else they infected. Without getting infected ourselves. We have to kill these things, but priority is getting people to safety. Understood?"

"Yes, Colonel," Symone and the rest were jacketed up quickly.

Manny's voice came through the com. "We got the alarm. I don't see anything yet."

As my facemask went up, I found myself grateful we were doing this in the daylight and not in the dark. It had to be easier.

"Ok, get your people on this channel. We need to be coordinated. How many Mobile homes did you manage to get moved?"

"About 80. 35 left. The word 'Mobile' is pretty euphemistic."

"Good work, though. How long until these 35 can get out of dodge?" I looked up at Rey

"I can get ten more out of here. The rest don't move at all."

"How many people left then?"

"42 people including Jamie, Myles, and our team." I looked around, there was no way we could fit that many in here."

"Ok, guys. Very quickly, let's try to usher as many people as we can in here and move them out." I pointed to Ladia, Rey, and Filo." You three will stay behind with me until they can get back with the rest."

Everyone nodded and we stepped out.

For a second, it looked like I was overreacting. Manny and Jamie managed to get 30 people stuffed in the Fearless before it couldn't handle another one. It would be tough, managing the weight, but they only had to go a short distance. Then get back and we'd take the rest.

I stood by the front track, rifle out. I had tucked one of those light guns in my belt and was waiting to use it. The key would be to kill the rat without triggering the drainer.

We had quieted the alarm and were trying to keep the noise down. Rats are attracted to sounds of movement, and I had no interest in attracting any of them.

That's how we heard it. I looked over at Filo. I think he heard it first. It sounded like a scratching sound with hundreds of fingers against a wall. I looked down at my foot and saw the ground start to give way under the starboard front track.

The Fearless was sinking into the ground.

I called out to everyone to clear but i was too close. The only way to avoid it falling on me was to try to grab on and climb up.

That instinct proved faulty as we dropped about 10 meters down, the track slamming into my waist and cutting me into two parts. My upper torso was thrown clear.

I lifted my head one last time in the dark and saw hundreds of rats advancing, their faces split, vertically, open to red maws filled with serrated rows of metallic teeth. A tendril wrapped around my neck and a million knives stabbed into my face as the cave under the mobile encampment filled with a million tiny red eyes then went black.

6- Menagerie

I looked around and thought for a second I had imagined that.

Rey was escorting some of the people into the Triage Bay door.

"Damn it." It washed over me. I lifted my foot and stepped away from the ship, grabbing Rey's arm.

"No." I shook my head. "Been there. This doesn't work."

It only took him a second to register. He lifted his mask. "Ok, what do we do?"

"Before anyone goes in, we move this thing. And we can't overfill it." I scanned the area, looking for the oldest growth tree. "There," pointing to it.

"Got it." He waved at the rest. I heard him give Symone the Details and the ship started moving toward the tree. The root network beneath it should prevent the Fearless itself from falling in. And we can keep the first group down to 20 or less.

We might be able to make this work.

Ladia came up next to me and dropped her mask, "What's going on. You ok?"

"Yea, it happened again. I died, then shot back into the past."

"Ouch."

"Yeah, that one really sucked. Don't look now, but this entire area is over a cave full of rat monsters."

"Oh, I don't like that at all."

"Really? I loved it." I grabbed her arm. "We need to keep track of all these people."

She waved Manny over. He was covered head to toe in old militia gear. "What are we doing?"

I pulled them both away from the area, "We're staying away from right there."

Ladia nodded, "cave full of rats."

"Do you have eyes on all your people?"

"I'm missing like 10 people. 2 trailers sank into a kind of sinkhole over there. Our people are trying to pull them out.

"Call them. Tell them to back away." I started running. The two of them followed. I could see the fallen trailers about 30 meters away. I tried yelling. At first, it looked like the scene in front of us was shaking, moving back and forth. Then, I realized that they were storming up from the open hole.

Rats.

The first ones to ascend were just regular rats. For a moment, I was hopeful. And then I saw the tentacles. They started ripping at the parts of the mobile home that were above ground. I felt the mud shake under me and I started sliding. The ground gave out and I started falling. The light sank above me as Manny and Ladia fell, too. We grabbed at each other and fell forward into a cavern. I could see the mobile homes up ahead with the rats sprawling over them. Most of the unchanged ones were trying to leave.

Mud poured down from above, filling my mask. I pulled it down and wiped my eyes.

Manny stared forward and started firing, "Motherfucker."

What I thought was a pile of mud launched itself at us, leading a group of people crawling through the cave, each one infected. They ran quickly, their limbs snapping and cracking in jerky motions. I could see that the animal in front of them was a dog. But it was changed. It was large, larger than a human. I stopped as a tentacle shot from its maw-like razor filled face, snapping my neck. Blood spilled from my mouth as I considered that I hadn't tracked any big dogs.

I missed this one.

***

The light flipped on, shocking me for a second before I realized I was standing next to the Fearless. I looked up and saw Rey. I switched the coms to universal. "All right guys. We're going to move the Fearless to the Big Maple tree about 7 meters in front of the picnic area. Look out for cave ins. People walk only in small groups. Everyone you can get to the ship. We have one trip."

Rey looked back at me and I nodded. He nodded back and started escorting the Fearless toward the tree.

Manny ran over, "We have…"

I put my hand on his arm. "I know. You have two trailers down in that sinkhole. The people are gone. They're dead. We have to move on."

"You can't know that."

"I do. Manny I do. Just like I know that the ground under here is full of rat monsters. You have to trust me."

"Those are my friends."

"They're gone, Manny." I pulled him along with me to the tree.

He wrenched himself out of my grasp and made it on his own.

I waved the team on and we assembled at the Triage Bay doors, at first glance, it looked like we had brought on about 25 people.

"Do you hear that?" Ladia met me at the doorway "That sound?"

It was the scratching sound.

"We need to get the fuck out of here and light this place up."

"Agreed."

We climbed on and closed the doors.

Manny met me at the storage space doors in the center. "Do you mind telling me what the fuck that's all about?"

I grabbed his hand. "In the back. Now."

"I don't work for you. Why did I leave my friends behind?"

"In the back. I'll tell you everything."

He turned and marched through the center corridor. Filo was already there. "Just listen, man."

"No, YOU listen. Those were your people, too. I've got like 10 people unaccounted for. And I'm supposed to take her word for it that they're just 'gone'?"

"Yes, you take her word for it." Filo stood up taller.

"Those are your people, too, man."

"I know. I know."

Rey's voice came over the coms, "You ready?"

I looked at Manny and Filo. I closed my eyes and took a breath, "Light it up."

"Roger," Rey signed off.

"Fuck you." Manny spit on the ground in front of me.

"Hear this out, man. It sounds crazy, I know, but it seems real." Filo grabbed his brotehr's arm.

"What are you going to tell me?"

I looked at him. "I died out there. Twice. You died once. We lost. And something is happening to me where, when I die, I snap back in time and sometimes I can fix it."

Manny shook his head. "Bullshit."

"It's true, man. I don't know how. We're trying to figure it out. She knows things the second time around." Manny looked at his brother in disbelief.

"Like I knew your people in the sinkhole were gone. Some giant dog had gotten infected." I tried to keep eye contact.

"Dog. Dog. Fuck."

"A big dog, bigger than a person. I wasn't tracking him."

Manny let out a breath. He seemed to deflate. "Hamburger. He's a Newfie. I didn't list him with the small animals."

"Because he wasn't. I didn't catch it, either. It's not your fault. It's not anyone's fault."

Manny sank into Filo's arms and started to cry. I motioned to Filo.

We had a lot to do.

***

Manny and Rey made sure everyone was comfortable in Triage. We had some runover into the back area as Symone drove.

The rest of us moved into the Lab.

Ella sighed. "It's a Nucleocytoviricota. A giant Virus. It's Megaviricetes class. Most viruses only contain a few genes. These are huge viruses that can contain massive amounts of DNA information. This one is about the same as the Pandoravirus Salina. It is 2.5 million nucleobases long."

I looked at the holo. Compared to other viruses, it was massive. "How many genes is that?"

"Well. A gene is about, give or take, a thousand nucleobases long."

Filo jumped in, "2,500 genes? For a virus?"

Ella looked over at me, "A regular virus might have ten to twelve genes."

So, this thing could replace, like a tenth of human DNA?"

"More." Ella looked deflated, "There's just no way to reverse any of this. It's just too big. It has significant phenotypical implications. It's a permanent change."

"El, Do you think the drainer has some impact on the incubation period?" Ladia looked through the notes on screen.

Ella nodded. "I'm sure it does. I mean the host is already infected. "

I looked around the lab. It was nearly impossible to tell that the Fearless was in motion. The shock protection system was really impressive. I thought for a second.

"How do the drainers do it?"

"They sort of don't. The drainer reasserts the baseline DNA of the host constantly. " Filo was becoming an expert at these devices. "If they change, it can't do that."

"And they filter toxins, too?"

He shot back. "Yep. They filter drugs, etc."

"And so they keep filtering toxins even after the host changes?" I had a glimmer of an idea in the back of my head.

"I think so. It's also a tracker. It's still functional. filtering out toxins." Filo answered.

Ladia looked over at me. You have a dumb idea, don't you?"

I breathed in. "It's super dumb, actually. Do you guys know anything about ototoxicity?"

***

I tried to stay out of Manny's way as we dropped his people off a few miles over. I think he had forgiven me, but he didn't need to see my face anymore. We did a quick sensor search of this encampment and found no evidence of drainers.

I wasn't sure what we would have done if we did.

"Tell me there are no rats on board." I slumped into the back couch. Rey was trying to assemble breakfast.

"I can tell you that. Definitively."

"You know, when I was a kid, back home, we had a rat sneak in one winter, while we were moving a couch inside. It took months to get rid of it. Literally. I hated that thing. It actually ate the working parts of the stove."

"Yeah, they try to stay warm. They are natural parasites."

"I hated that thing." I repeated.

"All right then. Rat free breakfast." Rey walked over to the couch with a plate of egg sandwiches. This was something I was learning about Rey. He was a natural nurturer. He was a leader. And the part of leadership that took care of its people he embodied completely. I took one and made a point to try to channel that more.

Ladia walked over with a couple of bottles of orange juice and passed them around. She leaned into the couch next to me and grabbed a sandwich.

"So, Ella and Filo... Something is happening there, right? Am I imagining that?"

Rey sat at the table. "Really?"

"No, you aren't imagining that. Those two crazy kids. I think they're both too smart for anyone else."

"Why am I the last one to see these things?" Rey asked, chewing.

"You're British. You have other superpowers." Ladia looked over at me, staring.

I pulled back, looking back at her. "What?"

"So, hey, if you choke to death on that orange juice, are you going to come back to life, go back in time a minute and be like, "No, grasshopper, I will have the apple juice instead?"

"Probably. I do like apple juice. Less acidic."

"Got it. Are we done investigating this thing or,,,"

"How do you suggest we investigate it?" Rey leaned in.

"Well, I don't. I'm not saying I have an idea."

"Do you want to kill me and see, Brutus?"

"Does anything else make you go back in time or just dying horribly in a pool of your own blood and poop?"

"What? Why poop?"

"Don't people poop when they die?"

"I do not remember."

"What if sleeping makes you go back a day?"

I took a bite of the sandwich. It really was good. I realized that I hadn't slept since prison. I wondered what the beds felt like in back. "I don't know. I mean, I haven't slept yet."

"Have we considered this?"

"Oh, fuck. I do not want to relive this day."

"She may have a point. I can't believe I'm saying this but isn't that how these 'living the same day over and over' type movies work?" Rey started pacing. I was starting to get to know all his ways of doing things. He was a pacer.

"I guess all I can really do is go to bed." I wasn't lying. The possibility of reliving this single day was excruciating. But it did make me think: What would I do differently? I took another bite. The little burnt crispy part around the egg was amazing. I hoped that if I did lose this day I would at least remember that much.

I got up and sighed. As I stepped through the bedroom door Ladia called out. "Not for any reason but I love you."

I turned. She had cheese on her face. " Well, not for any reason, but I love you, too." I looked over at Rey. He was looking nonchalantly up in the air.

"I love you, too, Rey."

He smiled, "Thank you, Colonel. Love you much. Get some sleep. Maybe it'll be a new day tomorrow…"

I slipped into the lower back bed. It was impossibly comfortable. I thought about what Rey said. Maybe it would be.

Or maybe not.

***

I woke up a couple hours later to find Ladia at the table putting together one of the light guns.

"Is that safe, there, madam curie?" I sat across from her.

"Oh, is it today now?" Ladia laughed. She pointed to the inside of the muzzle of the gun. "You see all this part?"

"Where?" I looked closer.

"Yeah, don't fucking bother, I can't figure that shit out, either."

"You hate that." I grabbed a box of crackers and popped one in my mouth.

"I hate the idea of carrying a weapon that I don't have any clue how it works. Do I just assume it's magical?"

"Maybe it is." Filo and Ella came in through the center corridor trying to pretend they weren't just holding hands. Filo looked in better spirits. "I'm really sorry about Manny…"

"Don't be. I get it, trust me." I got the sense thst Manny was the emotional one of the two. When he got Angry, Filo backed away. "We made some progress." He placed a disk down in front of me.

I looked at him. "Homemade?"

"Yes. with a couple of our own updates. This one is on a different frequency than theirs. As well, the functions of poison filtering and DNA reassembly are separate."

"Very nice work, teacher's pet. I destroyed a gun." Ladia handed the pieces to Filo who started putting the light gun back together.

Ella grabbed a bowl of cereal and began eating."We have no idea how much time we have after infection. It could be a few minutes. It could be a week. Literally no clue. I'm working on a vaccine, trust me. but if someone gets infected, this should help stop it."

"And if you wear it before you're infected?"

Filo sniffed, "Nothing. Nothing at all. It'll just filter toxins. Which is still useful."

Ladia sniffed, "Unless you're trying to enjoy your day off."

"Ok, I like it, but let's test the living bejeezus out of these before we have to use one."

"Agreed," Filo handed Ladia back her gun, assembled.

"You two make a good team over there," Ladia took her gun and tried to look innocent.

Ella looked at me, "That obvious?"

"Oh, my god, don't make me pretend." I tried to get a cracker in my mouth.

Filo looked confused, "What?"

Ladia put her hand over her face comically, "Does he know?"

Ella grabbed her hand, "Yes, he knows I like him, he likes me, we kissed. Ok.? Do you want us to fill out HR forms?"

"Yes. I absolutely want you to fill out long, involved HR forms detailing exactly how you feel about each other in triplicate. Then we will find a notary." I ate another cracker.

"I may stay out of this." Filo grabbed his drainer and slid it in his pocket.

Ella pointed. "I hate everybody in this room. Except him."

"I feel really special." Filo admitted.

Ladia started taking the gun apart again, "Well, enjoy it."

"Please do not kill yourself with that thing." I had an image of Ladia cleanly slicing her own head off with a light gun. Then it's me filling out forms.

Rey walked into the room briskly. We're here. Harbor Beach. Did you get some good sleep?"

"I did."

"And you arrived in today, right now, with us?"

"Apparently. Yes. The world does not reset when I go to sleep."

"Good to know. That's the good news."

"Oh, fuck me. There's bad news?"

"Yes." Rey stood up straight. He cocked his head and looked at Ladia dismantling the gun. "We should go to the other room for this."

***

Symone raised her hands, "between you and me, I don't want to be the one who is constantly showing you bad news on a monitor screen. That's not how I want our thing to go."

"Oh, I get that. No one likes to be the Vanna White of horrible shit. But, yes, proceed, Ms. White."

"So, we drove here, to Harbor Beach, obviously, hoping to make this trip to Ontario underwater where no one but Spongebob and Patrick can bother us. But, on a hunch, I went looking and I found:"

She wavered at the monitor and I saw a school of fish. They seemed mostly normal until we moved along to the last one. It was slightly bigger than the others and its face had opened along a vertical line, revealing what seemed like a rotating series of pins on a circle like spinning wheel inside a blood red maw. Its teeth were black and deep and tentacles shot out from the corners of its mouth, pulling in the fish in front of it to be devoured.

"Well, isn't nature fun."

"What's weird is that there are not that many of them. They don't seem to be infecting the others, just, well, eating them." Symone was pointing to another one. "It's weird. It's not like the Grand. Just one or two big ones."

"They look to be moving differently?" Rey offered up.

He wasn't wrong. Where other infected animals moved quickly, with cracking limbs, accentuated movements, in a rabid and excited way, these fish looked casual. They didn't look infected. Just different. But they still had all the visual characteristics of infected animals.

"What's our plan B?"

Rey cleared his throat, "Well, we make it to Windsor. Which means we go through Detroit. The most regulated and visible crossing point on the whole border. Through a single bridge. We would have no chance."

He was right. There was no way to make it through Detroit to Windsor. And the hours it would take us to get there were hours we didn't have, either. Hours we'd be exposed to American Forces. I opened the comms. "Does anyone have anything to say before we take this ship into Lake Huron with the infected fish?"

There was a second of silence. Then Ladia's voice rang out.

"Everyone back here thinks that's a super bad idea. Over."

7 - Huron

Symone kept her eyes in front but cheated toward me. "You really want to drive this thing, don't you?"

"That obvious, huh?"

"Would you like to take over? We have about two hours still."

"You know, I'm kind of an air slash ground person. I think I'll let you handle the other two elements for now."

"So, wait, I'm flying through fire, too?"

"Eventually. I'm just saying be ready, torch."

"You know, I had always noticed, in Zombie movies, that everyone is so worried about killing zombies and staying alive that no one ever really looks for a cure. Or a vaccine."

"Do you like monster movies?"

"I do. Not exclusively. But I'm familiar with this genre."

"Well, that's not this movie. In fact..." I fingered the comms on the front of my grey uniform shirt. "Ellabella. Kiss and Tella. Any progress on that vaccine?"

Her voice rang out over the system, "I will report on that when we are all done making fun of me."

"Well, I'm probably done." I looked at Symone. "You?"

She considered for a second and then responded in her accent, slightly less robust than Rey's, "I hadn't really started, actually."

"Ok, any rate, It's not aerosol or airborne. Too big. Definitely vector-borne. A bite. Stingers are mostly too small. I could build filters to keep it out, it's so big. But here's the thing. There are two parts to this."

"Ok, I'm listening."

"The first part is a standard giant virus package. It has its own invasive genotype. That includes the characteristics we've seen. Enhanced senses, compartmental vertical mouth, tentacles, rotary metallic teeth structure…"

"Yes, metal teeth. How is that a viral function?"

"It's an attracting effect. Iron and trace metals are drawn in and enrobe the bones. It creates a sort of internal weight supporting structure to cover for the 'muscle-snap' that we see, muscles becoming lean and naked, without a fatty coating. Bio metal coating."

"So, metal covers ALL the bones?"

"Yes, we just see the teeth. But that's not my big discovery."

"It sounds big to me." And it really did.

"The other part of this is a virophage, a smaller virus that activates it and creates the 'zombie-like' functionality. Virophages have a parasitic relationship with the co-infecting virus."

"Wait- Ella?"

"Yes, Symone?"

"The fish that we are seeing here in the Hudson. They seem to have the characteristics physically but not the rabid zombie qualities." Symone had been watching them longer than we had.

That made a lot of sense to me. "Right. Could they be infected with the giant virus but not the virophage?"

"It's possible. It would help if I had one to test." Ella asked.

I was afraid of the answer. "You want one of those fish as a sample?"

"Yes."

I dropped my head. This was the kind of stupid call that people made in movies all the time. Or it was our breakthrough.

It was hard to tell which.

***

"I don't love this." Rey stood in the lab with us, his arms crossed, staring at the center side wall.

"Do you want to veto it? I'll stop it if you say." I half hoped he'd say yes. In a hundred ways, this was still more his ship than mine.

Rey sighed. "No. It's your call. I won't deny, too, that I would probably make the same one. We can't just flail around without real knowledge."

"Yeah." I looked over at Ella and Filo, leaning against the lab table. "So, how do we do this?"

Filo pointed to the wall, "so, here, right behind this screen is the port side storage pod extending past the hull. It's lab storage. It's a mirror of the Triage Bay storage starboard side. And it's meant for things that we might need to jettison at any time. It's currently empty."

Ella tapped the storage under the table." I stuffed it all under here."

Filo continued, "Now, we can open the pod whenever we want, outside. We can jettison the pod. This screen can be made impermeable. It's not glass. It's a series of tiny cameras that project on the surface. We can store it in this area, like a bulletproof aquarium. It won't be able to touch us or hurt us or anything. We'll be totally separated."

"Ok, I like that. So how do you get genetic samples, etc." I put my hand on the screen. It felt like any other part of the wall of the ship.

Ella waved her hand over the sensor on the table. The screen area seemed to turn transparent, showing the empty pod within. She fiddled her fingers and I could see a series of tubes and devices that looked as though they could manipulate and hold a sample. "We do this. And we never need to touch it."

"And all of this is really strong? Unbreakable?" I really wanted to not worry about this. But no one was making that easy.

"Well," Filo started, running his hand over his curly hair, shaved all around. "Unbreakable. We don't really like to use that word, as an engineer. I mean I don't. But it's super close."

"Right." I stared the two of them down. While hers was a bit longer, fluffier, more wild, the two of them had nearly the same hair, both deep black. And despite Ella's black skin being a few shades darker than Filo's creamy latin skin, they both had the chiseled cheekbones that would make them stand out anywhere. They were a good looking couple. And was I giving in right now, in part, because they were so damn likable, so passionate? Was I being conned? I looked at Rey.

He shrugged. "Well, that covers my objections."

"Welp." I started, "Let's go fishing.

***

It took about twenty five minutes for one of the infected fish to swim into the storage space. Filo heard the buzz first and snapped to, closing the outer hull opening.

"Got you." He looked over at me and Ella. I had no idea what we were going to learn, but whatever it was, it was more than we knew now.

Ella used the machinery to reach out and snare it. It started to flail.

"Shit." I looked closer, "Is it in pain?"

"It shouldn't be. I'm not doing anything." Ella let the fish free from the tiny clamps and it seemed to calm down. It fluttered in the tank. There was another fish, a grey one, captured with it. Two tentacles reached out from its mouth and captured the other fish, stuffing it almost politely into its maw.

Filo was fascinated, "Wow. Did you get anything?"

"Yep, I got scrapings. Look at this. Ella moved down the table and loaded a small container into the microscope.

"We're being safe, here, right?" I was way more nervous about things like this than about combat.

"We are, but…" Filo fingered his com badge. "Hey, Rey, we're on alert back here, we have the specimen."

Rey's voice rang out, "Got it. Roger."

"He still thinks my name is Roger," Filo whispered to Ella.

"Isn't it? I thought it was, too. Fuck. This thing isn't infected."

They circled the microscope as I took a closer look at our fish friend. It began to shake and spit up on the clear hull screen. I reminded myself it was really spitting up on a series of cameras.

Then it hit me. Electronic Cameras. "Ok, guys, let's get rid of this thing now."

"What is that?" Ella stood up straight.

"It's like a liquid metal. "Filo reached for the button and the fish went spinning back out into the Lake. He leaned into the panel and it glowed with blue sparks before it exploded inward, sending shrapnel into him like tiny bullets. I saw him choke, falling to the floor. His neck was peppered with holes and the water pouring over him swirled with red.

He gasped for air. The room filed with the blares of alarms signaling a hull breach.

"Fuck." I grabbed Ella and tried to pull her away from the port wall. Another explosion rang out, this one followed by a wall of water. We were at the bottom of the lake. I looked at the gauge in the wall as I fell below the water. We were one hundred and twenty meters below sea level. Each 10 meters of depth adds 1 atmosphere of pressure, so, by the time the water had flushed the air from this room, we'd be at twelve atmospheres unaided.

I held onto Ella. She was trying to get to Filo, But I needed her to stay above the water. I pressed my comms badge, yelling over the alarm, "Rey, can you seal the hull?"

"I'm doing it. Not fast enough."

I pulled Ella, swimming toward the clean room. I could still save her.

Which is what I was thinking when a chunk of the hull sliced through my neck, severing my head.

***

It was bright. My eyes needed to adjust but I could tell I had no time. "What?" I looked at Ella.

"I said, it shouldn't be in pain. I'm not doing anything." She let the fish go and it quickly ate the smaller grey fish.

"Filo, eject this, now." I looked down for the button.

"Did we get anything?"

"Listen to me. Get rid of it, now. " I looked up. The fish seemed to stare me in the eye. It spit right at the cameras inside the panel, a stream of mercury-like liquid metal.

"Down," I grabbed Filo and pulled him back, away from the wall as it exploded.

"What the fuck? Ella looked at me. I could see the blood on her cheek from shrapnel from the explosion. She was breathing hard. I was counting in my head, waiting for parts of the hull to give way and slip into the lab and kill me. I yelled out at Filo, "Get to the clean room." If he could get in there, all I would need to do was get Ella to safety. The alarms blared over our voices.

"Give me Ella," I could see her panicking. The left side of her face was a mess from the explosion. She was in shock. I pushed him. "Just GO."

A piece of the hull came in through the opening and slammed into his chest.

"Rey," I yelled out.

"I'm getting the hull sealed. 30 seconds."

I felt the hull piece slam me in the back of the head. The last of the air in the room was being pulled out the hole over the water, which was filling the room floor first. I tried to grab the edges of the hull but I was pulled out. I shot into the water like a bullet. I felt my chest compress. My ribs cracked as I let out all the air I had in my lungs. I lost track of the ship. The alarms fell away as the space in my ears collapsed, rendering the world silent. I felt my head expand as my sinuses filled with water and explode. My head felt giant and then snapped back as I felt my skull break. The light turned red and then black.

***

I opened my eyes to hear Ella speaking, "It shouldn't be in pain."

"Both of you, drop to the floor. Crawl to the clean room, now." I pulled them down with me and we crawled quickly the few meters backward to the cleanroom. Filo opened the door and pulled Ella in.

The hull wall exploded and a wall of water began to fill the room.

"Shit." Filo and Ella moved into the clean room. I pulled out the light gun I'd been carrying around. I hit the door seal behind them and backed against it. The water was filling up so fast.

"Rey," are you sealing the room?

"It's coming as fast as I can."

"Faster, please." The water spun around me torrentially. I grabbed onto the zero grav handle near the door and hung on. I looked around but couldn't see anything to tie. I reached down and pulled off my belt, wrapping it around my arm and the metal handle.

I could feel the current trying to rip me out of the hole in the wall. The piece of the hull slammed into the wall separating the lab from the triage area, narrowly missing the storage space in between. The water was up to my neck now and my legs were being pulled out from under me. I lost my grip on the handle and the belt wrapped around my arm pulled tight, cutting off my blood sypply. I looked up. My feet comically tried to gain traction as the current kept swirling, yanking my feet forward.

The fish was moving toward me in a straight line. Hull integrity alarms were blaring and it was swimming directly at my face. I felt for my gun but it slipped under the surface and I lost it in the current spreading out through the room.

I took a deep breath. I had no idea what that fish would do to me. It somehow looked a lot bigger than it had. I reached over to untie my belt as the alarms went silent. The fish exploded into a paroxysm of light and metallic fluid, spraying into the water just inches in front of my face.

As the water started to recede, I looked up at Ladia. She had made the shot in the second after the center corridor door was finally able to open after the hull sealed. She glanced down at the light gun in her hand and back at me.

"I think I know how this thing works now."

Rey stepped into the back room wiping his hands. "Well, the lab is a mess, but the hull integrity is restored."

"Thank you." I realized I was pacing now. Rey looked at me concerned. "You ok?"

"Not at all."

"So, you had TWO time jumps. You did the same thing over three times." Ladia was really trying to get her head around this.

"I can't explain it to you, but, yes. I died twice. And so did both of you." I pointed to Ella and Filo, who were sitting together at the table holding hands. Part of me was grateful that they didn't have to see the other one die. Who am I kidding? All of me was grateful.

"And then you shot backwards what, like 5 minutes?" Rey looked like a man who was sure he could make this make sense.

"Less. I think both times I had maybe a minute, maybe two. It's not much."

"Well, it's still an advantage. We're still alive." Ella was more shaken up than I'd ever seen her.

"You only had two minutes." Rey was one of the those people when confronted with insane things, tried to break them down into pieces. "And you two were there and you don't remember?

Filo shook his head. "No. All I remember was the Colonel telling us to drop to the ground and get to the clean room. Looking back, I think that was the only way we could have made it."

"It was." I looked at him.

"So, this time jump gave you the chance to try out different solutions and choose one."

"Well. I wouldn't really put it that way. But, yes."

"So it's a win for us," Rey sounded final.

"It's a weird thing that helps us," Ladia offered.

"Look, whatever you say. Between you two, you saved me from a killer fucking fish."

"I didn't get much from it." Ella looked apologetic.

I thought for a second. "Wait. You did."

Filo squeezed her hand. "I think a lot of the research is ruined.

"But I remember. In the first timeline. You had a few seconds more to examine it. You said something."

"What did I say?"

"Ok, I remember. I don't know what it means. But you said that the fish wasn't infected."

Ella scrunched up her face and rubbed her eyes. "Ok, primary timeline Ella, who died, but let's not focus on that. She said that the fish wasn't infected."

Rey followed up, "But… It shares the characteristics of the giant virus DNA genotype. Did I get that right?"

Ella closed her eyes. "Yes, you did. That's exactly right.

"So if it isn't infected with this giant virus, it's a fucking crazy-ass coincidence that it looks the same and has all the same parts, including the creepy tentacles?" Ladia opened a bottle of water and drank. I think I wanted to stay away from water for a while.

Filo and Ella seemed to hit on it at the same time, "or…"

Ella continued, "the fish. Is the genetic template for the virus. They made the large virus package out of the fish's genotype."

"A fish that isn't from here. Alien."

Filo looked around the room, "They brought the fish here so they could make the virus out of it, triggering the whole package with the virophage."

I pressed the comm badge, "Symone?"

"Yes, Colonel."

"How dense are these fish out there? How many?"

"I'm really not seeing many. My guess is that there are only about twenty or so per square kilometer."

"Could these be grown versions of the smaller ones we saw in the grand?"

"Absolutely."

"Ok. Let us know if the situation changes."

Rey sat down at the table. "The Americans got these fish somehow and they are using the bodies of water on the borders to incubate them so they can build their virus."

"How safe are we down here?" I looked around the room.

"I think, as long as none of those things get near electronics, we're fine." Filo nodded.

"And there are no exposed electronics on the hull. Nothing"

"Oh, and Colonel, I meant to tell you." Symone's voice rang out over comms again,

"Tell us what?"

"We crossed the line. About three minutes ago. We are officially in Canada."

Everybody cheered. I looked across the room and tried to take in what had just happened. It felt insane to say. But here it was anyway.

"Ok, guys, we have a couple more hours. Let's get some rest." I slid onto the back couch.

"And tomorrow. We get to work."

8 - Tobermorey

Port Albert was not much larger than the Mobile home park, but considerably better organized. It housed about fifty Canadian regulars and had a number of ATARAS and other vehicles at its disposal. It was under the command of a sprightly Colonel Lemari-Ahmad, an easy-going British man of about fifty who seemed overwhelmingly happy to have us. He was even more excited by the information we brought.

After a lengthy debriefing, Filo and I showed the Colonel the aggregator. He shared the specs with him and his people and I hoped they'd be able to duplicate it simply. It had become so invaluable to us in the time I'd been on the Fearless. We also left a set of the light guns and the scanner that had shown me the extent of my own temporal displacement. I struggled with how much to disclose to the Colonel while we were his guests. After consulting with Rey, I decided to spare him the concern over my post-mortem time slips. I just didn't know enough to really understand what was happening and I didn't need to be benched right now when this team needed me.

As I mentioned before, withholding information never sat right with me, for a number of reasons. But keeping my team safe took priority over everything.

And Tonight that team would sleep in real beds on the base, which was all I could really think about right now. I agreed to meet with the Colonel later and pulled Filo aside in the dining area.

"I'm working on the other thing you asked me about now and I think I see how to do it. But this…" He shook his head.

"This sounds crazy, I know, but it's just strategy."

"Permission to speak freely, Colonel?"

"Argh. Look, if you call me Tomi, it's going to be a lot easier to disagree with me."

"Thank you. Tomi. Killing yourself is the absence of strategy. It's like anti-strategic."

"Yes, ordinarily, I'd be sitting there saying that. But you know it's different."

"I don't know. I mean I kind of do."

"Do you believe me?"

"I do, honestly. You have this temporal anomaly that shows up on the scanner. And you know things that you couldn't know otherwise. It's just… My mind goes over the scientific implications, you know?"

"I agree. Does it mean the timeline can be changed?"

"Yes, that's where it starts. Now we have to think about aliens from 800 years in the future. Are they back here to change the timeline or to reassert the timeline?"

"They are giving the Americans tools to win the war. What will they do?"

"Ok," Now that this was in a hypothetical space, Filo seemed far more comfortable. "They are going to go colonizing. They got Greenland and Panama, now Canada, which is huge. Other places with strategic importance. . Maybe the whole world, eventually. "

"So America unites the world under one rule. The Aliens come in and take over from their old partner easily."

"Right."

"And we need all the help we can get."

"So, you want me to make you a device that will kill you, quickly and easily."

"Yes, because, we see, that this seems to be the way to trigger my time jumps."

"Maybe it's adrenaline. Or some kind of shock. I mean, are you really dying?"

"Filo. I'm sitting here telling you that I feel myself die. That last time, I got sucked out into the bottom of Lake Huron and my head imploded."

"And you felt that?"

"Every second of it."

"So you want something cleaner and less painful."

"God, yes."

Filo stood up. I could tell this was not something he could easily agree to. "I feel like this is a terrible idea."

I walked over to give him a hug. "I know you don't know me well enough to want to kill me yet." I rubbed his shoulders.

"Give it time."

He started walking to the door. I called after him. "One more thing."

He stopped and turned around. "Underwater, in one of the timelines, you died because you disobeyed direct orders to leave Ella with me after she was hit."

"I did?"

"That doesn't happen again. Ever. ok?"

He put his head down for a second. "Yes, Colonel."

"Oh, and try 'Piujuq."

"I'm sorry, what?"

"It's an Inuk word, where Ella and I come from. It means 'Beautiful.' Kind of a little nickname that makes her smile. Piujuq."

"Piujuq?" He looked up, committing it to memory. Then his face relaxed, He smiled widely.

"Thank you."

***

The mess hall at Port Albert the next morning was built just like Ionia. But it couldn't have been more different. We sat around a table near the far wall as soldiers and medics, doctors, nurses, and engineers came up to ask us questions, drop off some interesting article of food or just introduce themselves.

"This is delicious," Symone's British accent seemed to become more pronounced when she relaxed. I realized this was the most relaxed I'd seen her.

"So, guys, this is technically our first mission." I placed the papers in the middle of the table and pushed them toward Rey.

"Really? That seems wrong to me."

"I know. What were we just doing?" Ladia shoved an English muffin into her mouth. I could tell how much she loved being back home.

"Well, I guess the Canadian High command would like you to know that, as much as they appreciate your service so far, all that stuff didn't count."

"Huh. weird, because it seemed real." Ella looked to have recovered from yesterday. I wish we could have stayed here for a few more days, honestly.

"Apparently, we have something to see before we ship out. And here he is."

I stood up.

Colonel Lemari-Ahmad was a tall, pleasant man with a wide white grin. He had the posture of a man who'd served his whole life. He was actually very handsome and his hair was thick, just starting to grey at the sides. In a movie, I would have easily cast him as the commanding officer of this facility, someone people willfully scurried around, trying to make proud. He walked quickly and made it nearly to the table before he was noticed by the group, who all began to stand when he approached.

"It's ok, no need to stand. Eat. Eat up." He shook my hand vigorously and clapped Rey on the back, before sliding into a seat next to him. "How are you all feeling?"

Rey looked over, "We're fine, sir. Anxious to move on."

"And we appreciate that. I wanted to show you her before you left. I understand that you have all fought one, too?"

This I didn't expect, "Yes, it was... It was a lot."

"We lost seven men to this one. And we can't transport it. We can't do anything with it. All we can do is contain it.

"Did you get samples from it?" Ella asked, taking a sip of her coffee."

The look on his face told us what we needed to know. They had gotten nothing from their prisoner.

"Tell you what. You finish up here. I'll meet you in section seven before you go." The colonel stole a piece of toast from the middle of the table and stepped away. We waved.

Filo put his cup down and tried to act businesslike,"So, where are we going?"

I placed a couple of images down on the table. "We are going to Tobermorey."

"Beautiful vacation peninsula," Ladia interjected.

"Yes, usually, except that now, it's also an important base that nobody can seem to contact." I flipped the pictures so they could see.

"Isn't this like next door, basically?" Ella was imagining the map in her head. She wasn't wrong.

"It's less than two hours away. Sort of a sister base. And it's gone dark. No more information than that."

"Ok, then." Ella lifted her glass, "Taima."

Ladia and I repeated, "Taima."

Rey looked up, "What is that. Tay-may?"

"Oh, sorry. It's like a phrase that means, sort of, "Let's go. Like. We talked about it, let's do it."

"Got it." Filo raised his glass, "Taima."

***

Section seven was at the edge of the compound. To get there we needed to make our way through five different sets of fire doors. Every new security point magnified my sense of dread to see what they had found. I tried to prepare myself for it.

But I wasn't.

The cell at the end of section seven was large. It looked like it may have been a lab at one point, surrounded by three layers of bulletproof windows. Two officers stood in front of the glass watching. My guess is that they were watching for tiny cracks, prepared to separate the section from the rest of the compound if they saw one.

Prepared to die.

Inside the cell you could see all the lab gear piled up on the left side. On the right, in the center of the remaining fifteen or so square meters of space, sat a little girl in a grey dress, covered in bloody stains all over. If you looked closely enough you could see that the dress was probably originally a canary yellow cover and the grey was mostly dirt. Her hair was blonde and midlength with little bangs that a very young girl might cut for herself, risking the consternation of a doting parent. Her arm moved as she hunched over, looking away from us, drawing in a coloring book in placid but slightly jerky movements. The lights were low but they began to raise as we stood there, clearly activated by some kind of automation.

The officer to the right wore a badge that identified him as Aronas. I nodded at him. He looked back, whispering. "If the glass weren't there, she would notice you're there from the smell."

Ella whispered back, "Why are you whispering?"

The little girl looked up. She put the crayon down.

"Watch," he nodded his head and whispered back.

The little girl turned around and we could see her face full on. At first, she looked like a normal, if dirty and bedraggled eight year old girl. Her cheeks were smudged and dirty, but you might expect her to light up, seeing people come to visit her. Then the red line slid down her face and it opened, ripping her face in two in a vertical line from top to bottom, revealing a massive crimson-red round maw lined with steel-colored teeth. Tentacles erupted from the side of her face and under her arms, propelling her faster than we could follow against the glass with a thud, where she stuck to the surface of the glass and screeched.

"Holy shit." Filo was breathing heavily. He hadn't seen one yet.

In this timeline.

I looked back at Ella, "What do you see?" I needed her eye.

"There's no drainer on her. She was probably organically infected. Eyesight is poor, which makes sense. Hearing is intensified.

Which also makes sense."

"Was she faking being a little girl still when we came in?" Filo looked confused.

Ella shook her head, "it's an instinct. The book was upside down. It's not real."

Ladia whispered, "In her head…"

Ella pointed. "Yeah. the mouth takes up the whole frontal region. No lobe. She's gone."

The girl was attempting to climb the glass now. She was grunting wildly, panting, and breathing hard.

Filo whispered, "Incredible."

Symone looked at Ella, "So why do you think it "makes sense," that the hearing is intensified?"

Ella waved her back. We started back through the doorway. The little girl heard us leaving and began to slam into the glass over and over. There were explosions of blood peppering the glass as we cleared the room.

I looked over at Ella as we left the room. For years, Ladia and I had worked to take sare of her, to cover for her and protect her. And it paid off in moments like this when the scientist in her pulled it all together. "Ok, spill. It's all relevant."

She nodded, "all right. I believe that the fish we found- the one that fucked up the lab - is the origin of the gene package for the giant virus that helps infect these…Zombies. It's the giant virus."

"I buy it. And…"

"I think that fish was an extremophile. Hundred and twenty meters down, dark. Notice that when her face opens in a flap, it doesn't prioritize her eyes at all? Light sensitive patches of skin, no functioning eyes."

"Like a fish from the bottom of the sea?" Filo offered.

"Yes. Extremophiles often have advanced hearing and Lateral line pressure sensitivity. - they respond to changes in pressure. Sound, too, is a pressure."

"So, you were right, before?" I thought about our conversation, and the bg dumb idea.

"I think so. They aren't sentient. They are vector driven."

Rey nodded, "just want to spread."

Symone took a deep breath. "They're sending us to Tobermorey because they think that one of these took it over?"

I didn't want to think about it.

***

It was hard to kick Symone out of the pilot's seat, even for a couple of hours, but I finally convinced her I needed to log some hours on this beast. My hopes that she would get some rest were dashed when she slid into the Nav pod next to me.

"You should go rest."

"I get nervous when I'm far from the rudder."

"I'm surprised you aren't more of a backseat driver."

"That's not me. Drive off a cliff. I'm fine."

"Don't tempt me. I'm better in the air anyway."

We were staying off the main roads but even so we could see the impact everywhere. Most of the people were staying indoors. The ones who were out were military, carrying guns, covered generally head to toe in body armor. I realized I'd been in Ionia for a long time.

I'd missed the explosion of this sickness, the infection now of these creatures.

It was light and the creatures were hidden away. But we were travelling through dense brush with tree cover. In places, the space in front of us was as cut off from the daylight as it would have been at night. After about an hour out, I pointed to the right, slowing the ship.

"Look."

About twenty meters in front of us, to the left, were five figures hunched over a group of bodies. They pieced through the bodies, stripping the meat off with jerky movements. I flipped on the infrared night vision on the right monitor so we could see. The door to the lab opened behind me and Ladia slid in.

"We stopped. Anything up?"

"Check it out." I pointed and enhanced the monitor.

Symone leaned in. The two in the middle are humans. A man and a woman. The other three are..."

"Coyotes? Wolves, maybe?" It was hard to tell. They were all covered in muddy blood, hair matted everywhere, limbs elongated and spider-like. The two humans looked as though they'd had the clothing and skin ripped from them.

Symone tried to figure out what could have made these five creatures into what we saw in front of us. She tried to write the story. "The Wolves, maybe, attacked the couple. Someone was infected. By the end, they all were."

"Should we be so close?" There was little fear in Ladia's voice. It was mostly an effort to do the job well - to behave reasonably in the face of danger.

I tried to make my guesses. I think they can't hear us or smell us through the hull. The Fearless runs smooth. And it doesn't really register as something foodlike. It's just big and metal."

I was fascinated by the way they fed. "Watch this. See?" The man in the center seemed to look around in all directions. Then, his face opened up along the center line and he ripped the meat from a large leg bone in front of him. The round red disk of his mouth seemed to rotate, letting the saber like silver teeth drill into the thick piece in front of him. Blood splattered everywhere and the bone was stripped.

Ladia leaned back. "What the fuck?"

"Did you see it?"

"I think so." Symone seemed hypnotized. "Right?"

"What did you see?"

"Before he opened his...mouth... before his face opened up, he looked around, he did a quick check."

"For what?" I asked.

It hit Ladia. "For danger. He was making sure it was safe."

"Do you think they are more vulnerable with their mouths open?" Symone asked.

I sighed. "I don't know. It looks like that's a possibility. Honestly, maybe I'm manufacturing something because I'm so anxious to have a win."

"Because they don't fight amongst each other. After they turn, they are the same. Human, animal, all of them. The danger is external."

Symone wasn't wrong. The five creatures seemed harmonious. Even organized. In a way.

"They're just giant extremophile fish. All they want is to eat."

I finished, "just not each other."

Ladia looked at me, "Are they poison to each other?"

I shook my head and shrugged, putting the ship back in drive.

I didn't know. There was so much I didn't know.

The three of us were quiet, moving through the dense forests heading up to Tobermorey. I hated dragging a team through some absurd mission without knowing more than I did. It had taken four of us to kill one of these things that was actually contained and we did it badly. What happens when we have five of them, or ten of them, in front of us.

Symone kept trying to contact Tobermorey on established channels. We weren't getting through. It's as if the entire facility didn't exist. We had other options, though, as we got closer.

"We're close enough now that I can patch into their internal comms."

"Okay, excellent. Maybe they still have internal comms. How many zones are we looking at?"

Symone checked the computer in front of her and turned back to me with a grimace. "It's thirty discrete zones. And it's not letting me tap into the global comm system. So I can run through, basically, thirty different rooms and try to find someone."

I kept my eyes on the ground in front of us. I could see the facility now. It was configured the same as Port Albert, almost identically. But it was torn apart. There were holes in the walls. "Let's do it. Room by room."

It took Symone sixteen tries to find the first occupied room. Two people. By the time she had tried all thirty, we knew what the size of the job would be. This would be a rescue job. To save the survivors left from the original complement of one hundred and seven.

five people. In three different rooms.

9 - Breach

Basic Military Officer Qualifications here in Canada require that you be, at the very least, bilingual. Every class has its own special stories, told by various mentors, about how speaking more than one language led to success in a situation, whether it's a better understanding of the situation from a native witness or confusing a monolingual opponent or any number of other situations that derive from speaking more than one language in a complex situation.

The target language is French, which is widely spoken across Canada. It is the first language for about a quarter of the people in Canada. Culturally, it means a lot and it's one of the official languages of Canada in pretty much every province. Most everyone I know can communicate in French. Even if we aren't fluent, we love it.

But Canada is big and has room for a lot of language. In fact, there is a common phrase I grew up with. "Uqausiq atausiq naammajuittuq" is something you might hear people say. It means, basically, "One language is never enough." My mother used to say it to communicate the idea that every perspective has value and we need to learn it, understand it, steep in it, if we want to see the whole thing.

One Language is never enough.

So, there are a number of inuit languages spoken here, too. "Inuk" covers a few of them. And, for those of us raised in it, it can be a really playful language, something used kind of joyfully.

I realized, as a leader, that there were benefits to it, words that tightly compressed complex ideas that could be shouted out when needed. Phrases that had come, through time, to mean far more than the pieces that comprised them.

One of my favorites, "Kajusitsiatuinnagit" basically means, "keep on doing that cool shit that you are uniquely known to do." It's a bit more of a pat on the back than "Keep up the good work." It's a recognition of the singularity and enduring nature of your contribution. There is an undercurrent that says, "You are not replaceable. Everyone knows it."

I like it.

To get a good idea of the playful wisdom and resilience of the language, try to wrap your mind around the idea of the "katajjaq," which basically means "song fight." Yes, the Inuit invented rap battles thousands of years ago. People with conflicts would write songs and get up and sing them back and forth, getting the community to understand their conflict and take their side. They were done (mostly) respectfully and in public. The work spent writing and practicing them gave people the chance to cool off. And an effort to be beautiful prevented violence.

So If I dislike this gun and would much rather meet some enemy in a modern day song duel, it's not some great secret why. To understand why what happened here is so upsetting to me, try to remember that this was the environment that Ella and I were raised in. We both grew up laughing through silly katajjaq and crafting poetic responses to disagreements. We grew up knowing we were only successful together. Words were important.

And this was the first time she ever swore at me.

"No fucking way."

"El, hear me out," I started.

"Five people, who might be hurt. Who might not make it back to this ship without an on-sight assessment."

"Which Ladia can give. And get right back to you so you're ready."

"So I sit here in this invulnerable box while you guys risk your lives."

"Right now, you and Filo sit here in this box that, by the way, is totally vulnerable, trying not to die, while you keep it safe, working on a cure. Because we don't survive two minutes out there without this box or you." I tried to pull back but I was already at an eight. I needed to really be at a six.

Rey walked into the tiger's den. "She's right, Doctor. As much as I want you assessing those people, too, we need to have a presence here, at the ship, to make sure it's not attacked."

"I fucking hate this." Ella looked deflated. But Rey's use of the word "Doctor" made it work. Hopefully it reminded her of where her responsibilities lay. One more time I mentally upgraded Rey's insights.

"I don't like the idea of splitting up, for damn sure. But the four of us are going to stay spry, huddle together, and try to hit three rooms, scramble back, and stay safe. Knowing that you guys are keeping this ready makes that possible.

"You're taking the Crovel?" Filo pointed to the sleek black metal weapon attached to my leg. One end of it had a sharp, thick crowbar while the other held a retractable shovel head, sharpened, that could be drawn in and out with a flick.

"Oh, yeah." He had missed how well this thing had served me when the guard had turned. I was taking it with me everywhere. "What do you got for me?"

Filo handed me a drainer he had made. And a little bag with the other eight. "Nine was the best I could do. It's the closest we have to protection."

I handed the bag to Rey. He took three out and passed them out to Symone and Ladia. Attaching his own to the back of his neck. The bag went into a utility pouch in the front of his vest.

"And..." He handed me the remote. "Patched into the two farthest rooms.

I'll have the movie playing."

Ladia interjected, "Which movie is it? Not that it matters."

"The film with the most audio dynamics in the library. Transformers: Dark of the Moon."

Symone winced. I agreed. Terrible film. But it wasn't for us. "I can turn it up, down and switch the room?"

"Yes." Filo pointed out the buttons. We could use their hearing against them, drawing them away.

"Now we just need to shut the fuck up."

Ladia smiled, "Easy."

It was light out still, which was comforting. I didn't anticipate too many problems getting from the forest line to the front of the facility. But it could be fairly dark inside, which wouldn't make our search any easier. Tobermorey looked as if someone had turned Port Albert into a cautionary tale. The brilliant rounded windows and curved walls at entry, starkly clear and white at Port Albert, here were cracked and awash with blood and dirt. The bright flags, welcoming allies and various humanitarian NGOS, so stately and beautiful at the other base were here, ripped and broken, colorless and drab, communicating no message, greeting no one.

We made our way quietly through into the foyer and I turned up the movie. We could hear the musical score, blaring out over people talking and mechanical effects. Filo had started it about halfway through so it began loudly already. I couldn't imagine what the creatures were thinking. Hopefully that lots of tasty people were hard at work above us on the other side of this building. I realized I needed to dispense with the idea that they thought ANYTHING. I was hyperconscious of the drainer on the back of my neck. It was scary, but not having one was scarier.

Like Port Albert, Much of Tobermorey was underground. So as we left the Foyer, we were in the best position we ever would be. Staring down at a series of levels through a large center area that exposed the floors below on a bridge connecting us to the main area. From here it resembled a large, sprawling mall. It even had a set of clear elevators in the center. Then I saw it.

I pointed at Rey and then down. At the bottom of the facility, about five stories down, was one of the infected. You could see the pieces of his torn uniform on his tall, lanky, extended frame. His mouth was closed and a serene look was on his face as he padded across the floor toward the noises. The four of us were holding our breath, trying to take in what we could.

He approached the door to the elevators and I felt my heart skip. We pulled back behind the well of a doorway and watched the creature reach out and tear off the elevator entryway with the tendrils snaking out from under its arms. It seamlessly lifted itself into the transparent shaft and began to climb. It was a quick and effortless ascension. The thing passed us without even looking at us. It looked like we lucked out as the enclosed shaft had possibly stopped it from smelling us. There was an eerie shriek as it reached the second floor above us, still visible inside the tube. It looked out and its face ripped open in the center, displaying the shocking wide blood red gap, ringed with metallic teeth. It was remarkably agile. Its eyes were dead and vacant.

Based on its Canadian uniform, I guessed this one was recent. I realized that there could be seventy or eighty of these here.

Everyone stationed at the base.

I took point and we moved down the stairs. Starting at the bottom was our best chance and that meant the two people trapped in the fourth sub basement. We hadn't been able to talk much since we ran the risk with every word of inciting the monsters, so we had no clue who they were.

I mentally marked the stairwell, in case it became harder to see later. The lights down here were missing in places but it was bright enough to see.

Two hundred and seventeen steps later, we reached D6, the sub basement room. I prayed they were watching the comm light in the room and pressed the button on the device in my pocket.

The door opened and the four of us slid in quickly to what looked like a lab. We locked the door again behind us.

The room was a mess. It was torn apart and what pieces of furniture that remained were upended against the doors leading in. A relatively short man with tightly cropped black hair in a uniform met us, alongside a pale blonde woman in a lab coat. I nodded at them.

The man looked relieved as he whispered, "I'm Lieutenant Rivas, this is Doctor Hull. Thank you"

Rey kept his eyes open, scouring the room as we introduced ourselves. Afterward he handed each a drainer.

"Where did you get this?" Doctor Hull looked as though she'd seen a ghost.

I looked over at her, "It's our version of a technology they invented. It's a drainer. If you get attacked and infected, it should stop you from changing."

"The one we were observing had one of these. They can be triggered, though."

Ladia stepped in, "Ours are on OUR frequency. They also filter toxins."

The two of them put them on as Rey got to business. "We have three more people to acquire in two more locations. What can you tell us about rooms C6 and A12?"

Rivas started prepping himself to leave, "You don't know who's in the rooms, right?"

"We do not." I watched Symone at the door. She nodded. This was going pretty well so far, I tried not to think.

The blonde doctor had looked tired and terrified. But she perked up.

"C6? That's right above us. Hold on." She made her way to the far wall and motioned us over. "Ok, so there is a vent here that leads to an airway between floors. There should be a similar lower vent in the floor in room C6- just offset a bit" She pointed to the floor where they had covered an air vent with a rug. It was about a meter forward from the vent above.

I looked over at Ladia. She nodded, "oh, I like this idea a lot."

Symone agreed, "anything that keeps us out of the hallways is a good thing."

Rey looked at the corpsman."Rivas? How high is the air passageway?"

He held his hand up, "About a meter and a half. We can move around."

The Dr. looked at me. It looked like she had taped up a bunch of junk over the vents. "I cobbled all this together. It seemed like they were smelling us, hearing us…"

"No, you're right. We need to make this very quick. We don't need our smell in the filters." I looked up. We could pile two tables together and tape them. That way, we could have a sturdy base to step up quickly and easily.

I motioned to Rey, "We'll just make this a simple stairway and get a line of us up and out."

"Agreed. Sturdy and quick." He and Symone started pulling the pieces together.

Rivas was trying to make sure the doctor was calm. I approached him, "ok, Rey's on point, then the Doctor, then you, Symone, Ladia, me. We're quick, we're quiet, we don't stop, ok?"

"Yes, Colonel." He made a motion to salute me and I pulled his hand down. It was shaking. "We're all going to be ok. Our ride is right outside." He nodded.

Rey pulled the trash off from over the vent and we started moving in a straight line. He was still struggling to open the upper vent when I climbed up. I realized the problem.

'The space between floors was seemingly endless. Thousands of square meters of open space, punctuated every once in a while with a padded blower engine to increase air flow. The space went on, seemingly forever, until finally closing up into dark pockets surrounding the entire area. It was hot and humid and I felt exposed. The real problem, though, was that every move, every breath, echoed in this space and reverberated to the far ends. We had to quickly move up.

And quietly, too.

"Rey..." I whispered.

"Almost there." I could see he very nearly had the vent opened and unblocked.

I opened my eyes wide. Nothing I could do would make that move any faster. Ladia tugged at my sleeve. She pointed. At first, I couldn't see anything. Then, I followed her finger.

Emerging from a pocket of dark far at the end of the space. A shadow seemed to move.

"Rey, now is good," I whispered.

I could see the sweat on his face as he turned and nodded. The vent was open. He pulled himself up, followed by the doctor.

I squinted to try to see the shape. It was moving toward us impossibly fast. It looked wide and flat, like some kind of sting ray racing across the floor of the space. I pushed Ladia.

Rivas pulled himself up, followed by Symone. I could see it now.

Rats.

As Ladia pulled herself up I saw the ruddy crimson flash of a tentacle.

These were infected rats. I dug my hands into the space around the vent and launched myself into the room above, without looking. The closest of the rats was only about 4 meters away. I pulled my feet up, as quietly as I could and rolled on the floor, pulling out the light gun. A black rat, face open and rows of teeth circling, propelled itself upward with the tentacles ringing its face. I shot across its head, cleanly removing the top of it. Two more rats jumped up before Rey dropped the metal desk down on its side, completely covering the vent.

The two rats scurried behind a mess of equipment as the one I'd shot flopped on the floor like a fish before lying still. I looked up and Symone pulled out another light gun, shooting over my head. The beam went through the head of another infected rat and punched a hole in the far wall. Rat number two fell to the ground, shaking, sloppily and died in a pit of blood.

"Careful," I whispered. "We don't need any new holes in the floor."

Symone nodded. I tried not to think about how much noise that had made as I stood up. To Rey's side were two clearly military caucasian men. The first held his hand out to me. "McGovern. This is Lucas. Security."

"Good to meet you guys." I was trying to follow the third rat but I was afraid I lost it. Rey handed the men drainers as I looked at Ladia. She was pointing at a space near the north wall, not far from the doorway out of here.

"I feel like I can hear them." Ladia pointed to the floor. I tried to listen but they weren't our problem right now. This third rat was.

I leaned in to Rey, "Can we flush it out?" I whispered.

"I don't know." If we had time, sure."

As it was, it would likely pounce the minute we opened the door to get out. "McGovern." He looked over at me. I tried to remember what I knew about situations like this and constantly give people something to do to keep their minds off what the fuck was happenning.

I raised my finger. "Shh. Can you draw a map out of here to room A12 on your hand? Lucas, Grab a lightgun and help us sweep for this thing."

Rivas covered the doctor as we tried to spread out in the room. I wasn't about to drag an infected rat with me to the next room.

Suddenly it sprung up and latched onto the wall, centimeters away from where Ladia pointed to it hiding, scurrying along the wall parallel to the floor. It seemed to stick to the wall like a spider, tentacles spreading out in front and propelling it across the wide white lab.

I shot at it with the light gun, grazing it and sending it skitterring to the floor. It seemed like it wasn't moving like a rat anymore. It had the lithe movements of a large predator.

Dr. Hull fell back against the wall, tripping on junk scattered on the floor. She lifted her arms as the Rat snapped its head in her direction, leaping at her. If I shot it, the doctor was right behind it, clearly in the path. Symone had a better angle. She let go and sheared off the animal's right arm and leg. It landed on the doctor and dug into her neck.

Rey spun and grabbed it with both hands, pulling it from her. Without its other arm and leg it couldn't grab on completely. He threw the rat across the room and with one motion I shot a beam through its head. The body continued on, flying forward until it slapped against the wall and fell dead.

I grabbed the crovel and moved toward the inert body. It was dead. An impossible amount of brownish red blood was pouring from the neck, still pumped by the dying heart.

Ladia and Symone held up the doctor. Rey had been quick but not quick enough.

There was a seven centimeter long gash in her neck where the rat had pulled the skin away.

She had been bitten.

10 - Alive

"It's going to be fine, doc. It missed the big scary arteries. It's all good." Ladia was trying to calm the doctor while I held her hand.

"I'm bit. I'm bit." Doctor Hull rocked back and forth with her eyes shut.

"Look at me. You have a drainer on, You're not going to change. Open your eyes." We still had over half of this mission. I needed her not to panic. Although, in her situation, I think I might.

Rey was explaining the drainers and how they functioned to the Tobermory people. I asked Symone to keep an eye and ear for anything. I started a timer in my head. I wanted to calm everyone and be out of this room in five minutes. Now it was a matter of filling those minutes.

"Doctor. You're going to be OK. Our own doctor is back working on a cure and a vaccine and we have the drainer technology. We can beat this. But you have to stay calm. Can you do that?"

"Yes. Yes. I can."

"Good. While this top-of-her-class nurse stitches you up, why don't you walk me through what happened here. It might help." I leaned in close to her. We had all become so used to whispering it was second nature now.

"Ok, you're right. Information is good, right?"

"That's exactly right. Can you tell me what happened here?" I tried to focus single mindedly on the Doctor.

"We shipped in. We were all in group A. We're supposed to be getting this place together to be occupied. Full complement."

"And how many of you were there?"

"About forty. Forty three, I think, including me. It's a skeleton contingent preparing for full occupancy."

"Good, good, better than I thought."

"And how many of us are left? How many here?"

I realized she wasn't prepped on the scope of our mission. I looked at Ladia, who shook her head. "It's five. You four and one more person in room A12."

A slow moan came from her throat, something ancient and unintentional. I realized that, as the doctor, she had probably done the physicals on all forty three of those people. All of them.

"We can get you out of here. We can. Can you tell us what happened next?"

"Ok. We moved in. We started…There was a girl playing in front of the base one morning. Just a girl about seven or eight. She seemed traumatized. She couldn't speak. I was the first to see her when they brought her. I couldn't find the cause of her muteness. She seemed in good shape."

"You ran tests on her?"

"We did. I did. I didn't find anything too odd. There was a metal disk attached to her. We thought it might be a tracker. I couldn't remove it without hurting her. We were going to send her to a children's hospital in the morning."

"A nearby hospital?"

The doctor looked up at me, her eyes were wet and her lids were heavy. I needed to keep her talking. Just for another minute or two. "Then what happened?"

"That night. She changed. No one saw it. But it was on camera. Something happened to her device and she changed. In less than 20 minutes, she killed everyone here."

"Did they change?"

"Some did. But she was hungry. And some she ripped through their spinal cord."

"And they can't change without a spinal cord?"

"Apparently."

"The monsters drink the spinal fluid if they're too hungry. It stops the new host from changing, though. They're just dead."

"That's good. Good to know."

"It can be transmitted through fluids passed through the stomach barrier."

"So don't get their blood in your mouth? Got it."

Ladia stood up. She had wrapped her neck wound. She carefully removed her gloves.

"Are you ok? Are you feeling alright? Can you walk?"

The doctor nodded and pulled herself up. Rey had organized everyone near the door. "It's the same layout as the floor below. We get to the stairwell and we go up."

We could still hear the movie playing from far off in the compound. I looked at the device in my hand and turned up the volume a tiny increment. It probably did nothing.

"Listen up, guys. There is no reason for them to be alerted to us. A lot of noise is going on below us and to the South. We are going up and north.

We'll be quiet, get to A12, back to the stairwell, to the bridge area, the foyer and out to the ship. We'll stick together."

Everyone nodded. I handed Rivas my light gun and grabbed the crovel off my thigh. I admit that it made me feel more ready to have a bludgeon of some sort on my hand. Against Rey's clear unease, I took point and we moved out the door.

The sounds from the movie were louder in the hallways. In the spaces they were broadcast, they must have been crushingly loud. We moved a single file to the starwell, hunched against the left wall. It felt safer only to have to protect one side. Symone checked the stairwell and we poured into it. We started moving up the first of two levels and everything was clear. The doors were locked and tight.

We made it up to level A before everything went to shit.

Right outside the stairwell it looked like a battle of some sort had happened. The walls were scorched and scarred, as if by fires. And the floor was gone, missing for almost ten meters, from wall to wall, with a tiny, maybe six centimeter wide ridge on one side all that remained of the entire floor of the hallway, riding over a seemingly bottomless darkened pit. A wall of stench surrounded the open area of the pit. It was oily and acidic, musky and sweet. It smelled familiar.

I looked to Rivas, "Do you know what happened here?"

He shook his head. It looked like all four of them had been stuck in their respective rooms during this fight. I motoned to Ladia and she pulled out the night vision goggles. I wrapped a cord around her waist and she moved toward the edge. Peering over, she grabbed at the rope and very nearly slipped. I pulled on it and grabbed her arm. I don't think I have ever seen her that shaken, ever.

"No. Just no. No fucking way. No." She handed me the goggles. I looked over at Rey. He was trying to find the right spot on the night vision recorder. He motioned me back and we all slid back onto the stairwell. I pulled the door shut. It was bent and wouldn't fully close, but it provided some protection.

He showed me. The hole went down to the floor below. If we had opened the stairwell on the B floor and gone into the hallway we would have walked right through them. It looked like twenty or thirty bodies, floating in blood and septic water. And crawling all over them were about one hundred giant cockroaches, each one between five and 20 centimeters long, with black brown tendrils snaking out from the sides of their blood red open faced maws, ringed with metallic teeth.

Giant Infected cockroaches.

Suddenly the smell made sense. It was the mass smell of cockroaches, coupled with the decay of the bodies and the iron-like smell of blood. The cockroaches must have drowned in the blood and turned, taking on the viral load of the infection. .

Symone took a deep breath. "If we see a hundred, there must be thirty thousand of them in this facility. That's the law of cockroaches."

That sounded hyperbolic to me, but not wrong. Under no circumstances do we go to the B floor. I turned to the Doctor, "Are you doing ok?"

She nodded. I was 100% sure that if she saw what was on that monitor she would not be so calm. I looked at the team. "Ok, guys, the ceiling looks untouched. So change of plans. We go up one floor and break into room 1-12, then pull our person up and get the fuck out of dodge.

Rey looked up, "The rats…"

Ladia shook her head, "I'll take the rats. I'll eat the fucking rats. Seriously. I love rats."

"You do not love rats." I reached for her hand

Lada shook her head vigorously "On a sliding scale, I fucking love rats."

"I whispered to the core team while the others stood just out of earshot. "Let's keep this to ourselves."

We moved up to the first floor.

Symone took point and opened the door. The hallway was clear. As we moved over the floor sitting right above the giant hole I felt what might have been a little give in the floor. I'm sure it was my imagination. Those massive things were infecting my brain. Every inch of me itched and my skull wanted to sneak out of my body and run.

Room 12 had a bright blue door, the kind usually designating a mess hall or kitchen in these compounds. Some part of my mind registered that as important. I used the crovel to pry the door open and we all slid through the half open door. I had meant to leave the door open for a fast exit, but these hallways were now a source of their own terror. Rey pulled the door shot behind us.

We needed to break through the vent, then through the lower vent, and pull our person free. I grabbed Symone. She and I would go down into A12. Ladia and Rey would keep watch in the airspace between and the rest would stay up in 1-12 and secure the room. The first part of that went like clockwork.

We didn't see anything in the space above the A floor. Not yet, anyway. I went first, grabbing Symone's legs as she slid into the room. It was getting darker and I couldn't see anyone. The room was wide and filled with chairs, couches and tables, like a lounge. I scanned quickly. There should be one person in here.

No one.

We moved into the room. There was a rusling near what looked like a communal kitchen area. I took a step forward and stopped. On the table were two of the largest cockroaches anyone had ever seen. They were both eating what looked to be rotten bananas from the top of the counter, each one easily as large as the largest ones we'd seen below.

I looked down. The feeling I'd had back in Hidden valley where the ground gave out. Suddenly it hit me. These areas were the food areas. They were all infected with cockroaches. Cockroaches that were making their homes in the floorboards, rotting the floor out, prepping it to fall through,

I stepped back and shook my head at Symone. She pointed to my left.

In the center of a counter, a cupboard door was half open, and a girl had stuffed herself in there. She couldn't have been more than twenty years old. She had an ensign's insignia on her ripped shirt.

Her breathing was unsteady and shallow. She motioned to me.

Be quiet.

I waved my hand for her to come over. Just then, I heard Ladia whisper from above, "guys, it's time now."

The girl moved toward me and I grabbed her around the waist. I tried to make sure my weight was evenly distributed and moved under the vent feeling for the rope. Grabbing the girl I dropped my crovel. In the silence of that space it sounded like an anvil dropping.

I felt the rope in my hand and grabbed tightly as it pulled me up.

The two cockroaches launched themselves off the counter and shot toward us. Symone sliced the closest in half easily with a light gun and Then grabbed the rope under me. She shot twice more as the girl and I slipped up through the vent. I I turned in the hollow space and saw a cadre of rats advancing, pushing the girl up through the upper vent and following. The skitterring of rat claws blended with the advancing carapace clacking of the cockroaches into an inhuman, alien machine noise. I grabbed at hands until Rey and Ladia came up through the vent into the first floor. Rivas and McGovern clamped aboard down over the vent and started piling furniture on top of it, while I fell back against a wall.

I nodded at Symone who kneeled next to me. "The floor collapsed. All of A floor is probably gong to fall through. I don't know what that means for structural integrity for this floor."

I was breathing hard. "Nothing good. We need to get out of here."

The film score continued. I looked at my timer. We had only been in this building for twenty two minutes. That felt impossible. Ladia and Doctor Hull looked over the girl as Rey handed her the last drainer.

She had been in that cupboard for two days, terrified, hiding from the infected. Cockroaches had their own sort of echolocation, which, coupled with the lateral line pressure recognition skills of the infected meant she had to be completely silent.

I realized that the floors could no longer be trusted. This added a bit of complexity to the rest of this mission. We pulled the ropes out and tied everyone firmly. We were going to have to move in order from here on, in a row, according to how we were tied.

Rey handed me his light gun, grabbing another from his waist and took point. I followed him. It was a straight line now to the outer doors and out of here. Right behind me was the doctor with Ladia behind her. Symone took back and we all tried to move like a single unit. As we made our way past the clear elevators, I tried to remember what shape they were in when we'd seen that infected earlier climbing it. It could have been my imagination, but i was sure they were more damaged, with the closest one sporting a waterfall like coating of blood on the inside of the tube.

Rey pointed left and we ran that way. It was marginally closer that the rightmost bridge. It was still dark below us, looking over the bridge, but now we could sense what was happening down there.

Now we knew.

My skin crawled as I imagined falling into that hole, knowing what was waiting for me on the floors below. As we started moving over the bridge I heard a creaking sound. I listened again to make sure it wasn't my imagination. It might have been the film soundtrack, full of metallic transformer sounds. As I moved in lockstep with the team and listened, suddenly my ears seemed to invert.

It was deathly quiet.

The sounds meant to distract the infected and pull them to the other side were gone.

I grabbed the remote and tried to restart them. But it wasn't the remote. It wasn't the soundtrack.

The infected must have destroyed the speakers in the rooms they were playing. I listened closely, again to the creaking noise. It grew louder. I looked up.

There must have been about twenty human infected climbing down the metal girders of the space above us, closing in on us. They were long, almost twice the height of when they were human. They looked like they had been fed. They were thick and bloated.

And heavy.

Two of them fell onto the bridge behind us, right in front of Symone. She pulled out her light gun and began slicing their heads off. They scrambled to get a footing on the bridge but the floor of that surface was weakened, too. Suddenly, I saw Symone's head fall below the surface of the bridge.

I tensed up, waiting for the inevitable pull from the rope and, sure enough, it came, strong enough to nearly yank me from my feet. There was no point in being quiet now.

"Everyone pull. Now. Forward. Move."

I looked at Dr. Hull behind me. I could see her start to shut down. I grabbed the rope behind her and looked her in the eyes. "We have to pull."

She nodded. I tried to ignore the infected descending on us as Symone's head appeared above the bridge floor. She pulled herself up and the rope became looser again as we all ran toward the entrance. I shot upward without looking up and when Rey slammed through the front door, I was right behind him.

I swore under my breath as I saw Filo standing right by the triage bay doors, open, and waiting. He had no business being out of the vehicle.

We raced toward it, pulling each other along via the rope that cinched us all together. The infected were just about 10 meters behind us when the door slammed shut after Symone flew in.

"Move, drive"

I reached in to touch Ella's leg as she sat in the Nav Pod, connecting door between us open. She looked like she'd been practicing driving. She touched my hand and squeezed hard.

I closed my eyes and heard Rey call out. "They aren't following. No one."

Filo cheered. No one else really had it in them.

***

As we got closer, Ella and Filo checked on Dr. Hull's drainer. I tried to talk to the young ensign, whose name was Aloya. My guess was that she wouldn't be alright for a good long time.

I pulled Rey aside. "Why is it dark?"

"I honestly could not tell you. If you want another mystery, the roads look different, somehow. And I can't get Port Albert on Comms."

"Filo, did anything strange happen while we were in there?"

"No, Colonel. I had to restart the movie four times. But besides that, nothing at all."

"Wait, why did you have to do that?" I glanced at him then back to Rey.

"Well, no big deal, but the move is only two hours long."

I took a deep breath. "How long were we in there?"

Filo looked at me confused. "Colonel, it's been about eight hours. I'm just glad you're finally out."

For the first time since I'd met him, Rey looked lost, "Eight hours? Are you sure about that?"

"Well, give or take."

I tried to make some sense of that. I hadn't lost time. I hadn't died.

What could possibly have happened? There was no way we were in there for eight hours. I walked back to the living space and sat on the couch. This thing had to make sense. I closed my eyes for a second.

It was only supposed to be a second.

***

Ladia woke me up, " We need you."

I shook it off and followed her out the Triage Bay doors. It was night and Colonel Lemari-Ahmad was standing there with two of his men and the returned complement from Tobermorey.

"Colonel, I'm sorry. I must have nodded off."

Rey spoke up, "We were going to let you rest, but you need to hear this."

I looked at the men. They looked tired, worn in the light of torches burning near the entryway.. Where before Colonel Lemari-Ahmad had been an easy going and personable man, he looked like he had been replaced with a sterner, older version of himself. He looked at me suspiciously. Too suspiciously, given that we had finished the mission and brought all five of the complement home.

"Is everything ok?"

"You don't have any recollection of where you've been?"

I stared at him, "We were at Tobermorey. We left this morning."

Rey rubbed his eyes and turned around. "That was a year ago, Tomi."

I looked at him. This was the first time he'd called me by my actual name. "Rey, what are you talking about?"

Ladia jumped in, "He's not lying. Somehow we've been gone a year."

Colonel Lemari-Ahmad rested his hand on his sidearm, "What happened out there?"

"I don't know. We left this morning. Right, guys?"

Everyone nodded. "Ladia stepped forward with Dr. Hull, "one way or another, we need to get the doctor some help. I dressed the wound, but it's just a field dressing."

The Colonel looked up. "What wound?"

The Doctor stepped up and lifted her head. Without missing a beat the Colonel drew his gun and shot her in the head.

Ladia dropped to the ground, holding the doctor. "What did you do!!? Why did you...?!! What did you do?!!"

I moved over in front of her and grabbed his gun. "What the hell did you just do? She had a drainer on. Why did you do that? What's wrong with you?"

"What's wrong with ME? Me? What's wrong with You? All of you. You disappear for a year and then bring back an infected? Look at this place. Do you think we've been patiently waiting for you for a year? What do you think happened here?"

He pointed to the group from Tobermorey, "If you want to stay with your doctor, here, you can. Otherwise, you're welcome to stay and help us rebuild."

He looked over at me and Rey. Behind me Ladia was cradling Dr. Hull's lifeless head. "The rest of you are welcome to go."

11 - Waaseyaagmiing

We parked the Fearless Outside the building for the night. It seemed the safest for us and Port Albert. Symone took the first watch, and while I felt rested the next morning I still didn't feel like we had any more information.

We sat around the table for breakfast as Rey came in from the center corridor, "Well, my connections at the UN confirm we've been gone for a year. They aren't too happy, either. And they seem reluctant to buy our time displacement story."

I looked over at Filo, "What do we have technology-wise that can prove it?"

"OK, we've been recording everything. You all have about thirty minutes of recorded activity from inside the encampment, Ella and I have about eight hours. None of us has a record from last year. So anyone digging through our logs here would know we're telling the truth."

"Thirty minutes I want to forget forever." Ladia scrunched up her face. Symone lifted her glass of orange juice and toasted her to that.

I absolutely agreed. "Would any of that help?"

Rey shook his head. "Maybe. I don't know. I'll give them full access. Let's see what they say."

"Well, This isn't the ending we had hoped for, but I will tell you that I'm very proud of all of you. Filo, that drainer worked perfectly..."

"For all the good it did." I could tell this was hitting Ladia hard.

Rey jumped in, "And the audio diversion was amazing."

"Definitely." I raised my own glass, "Sy, you saved my life at least twice, Ladia, you saved everyone at least a few times, Rey, you knocked it out of the park, And Ella, you two kept us alive at the end. I have no notes. Flawless performance."

Rey clinked his glass with mine and sat down. At this point, I think we all deserved a good meal. So, of course, the proximity alarm sounded. Symone reached over and pressed a button on the remote at the end of the table. The monitor wall sprang to life. It was Rivas, right outside the Triage Bay door.

I looked around. I grabbed Ladia and we made our way to the door.

"Nothing but him out there." Symone checked the sensors. I shrugged and opened the door. Ladia and I stepped outside. There was a slight chill in the air but it was a beautiful day. I reminded myself to stay on my toes, prepared for what might be outside. But that reminder didn't always feel real.

"I really wanted to thank you all. I'm sorry about all of this." He started.

Ladia shook her head, "It's not your fault. How is everyone else?"

"They are a little better, after a good night's sleep. But I'm confused."

"About what?" I realized I hadn't managed to debrief any of the Tobermorey people.

Rivas looked back and forth between us. "We lost a year, too. And I don't know where it went."

I considered for a second.

"Why don't you come in here and talk?"

***

Rivas explained the dilemma from his perspective. The Tobermorey attack happened just days ago, his time. That's when the distress signal went out, picked up by Port Albert. We arrived there a day later. In the memories of all the Tobermorey people, there was no year's worth of time that could account for our lost year.

Their account squared with ours.

Rivas had spent the morning reaching out to people he knew, finding many dead or missing, and the rest, who hadn't spoken to him in a year, wondering where he had been. The experiences of the rest of the group weren't too different. From what he told us, he had been fairly self contained his whole life. Except for the woman he had proposed to two months before stationed at Tobermorey. Her name was Daanis Ginew and she was next in line for security head at Waaseyaagmiing, or Georgina Island, another base not far away.

"She was going to transfer once we were set up. I talked to her last night. She confirms it. I've been gone for a year. She hadn't heard from me in a year."

"I'm really sorry." That was difficult to hear. I brought him a plate and sat down.

"But to me… Anyway, Wasagaming is under attack by those things and they are down to a skeleton staff. They need help." He pulled a usb out of his pocket and placed it on the table. "If you go, I want to go with you."

I looked over at Rivas. Sitting, we were almost the same height. He was muscular, with a long torso and short legs. He was probably about one and three quarter meters tall, a height that had surely forced him to work a little harder in the military. And I had no problem with his swift responses during the rescue.

"Ginew...Eagle, right?" I nodded at Rivas.

He looked honestly surprised. "Yeah, in Ojibwe. That's pretty good."

"It's a parlor trick. She's a language nerd." Ladia winked. She could tell I was in.

I looked around the room. Rey and Ella were nodding. "No one's going to say this is a bad idea?"

Ladia got up and grabbed a cup of coffee, "Oh, it's a terrible idea. We just all have extremely poor judgment. Even these proper British people here.

"I lost my judgment on that bridge, Guvnuh." Symone added, in a caricature of herself.

"Bella, can you give him a once over before we go?" I nodded at Ella who nodded back.

"Got it."

I grabbed the usb stick. "And can you run through this?" I handed it to Filo."

Glancing around the room, I realized that a mission may be what we needed right now. Something was gnawing at the back of my mind. And I wasn't sure I needed to give it air right now.

I paused. "Ok. we may be a bed down on the way, but we'll make do. Lieutenant, why don't you grab what you need and let's go.

***

Waaseyaagmiing was the native name for Georgina island. It was the largest island mass in Lake Simcoe, in Southern Ontario. Not long before the war started, it was ceded back to the Chippewas, Ojibwe First Nations tribe. Not too much had changed, though. It was still an important base, just one operating under First Nations law.

Now, let's dig a little deeper into that, because no part of the base actually touches the island itself. Georgina island had a population of about a thousand people. It's about 3500 acres- a bit too big for one contiguous base. But in the southernmost corner of the Island, between it and the connecting ports, Floating and reaching about 20 meters down, is the base itself.

It's three floors altogether, making it a bit smaller than both Tobermorey and Port Albert, but two of those floors are below the water line.

"Got it. I have questions."

Filo looked up from the holographic display. "Ok, shoot."

"Some of these are for you and some are for E. first up, how many people and is the base salvageable?"

Filo looked at Rey. Rey offered up, "We think it is. They have about twenty people and they are all sequestered in the top level. The bottom two levels are blocked off and are experiencing problems with infection."

Rivas jumped in. "We've been calling them Zeds. Or Zeroes. But they are Zombies. No doubt."

"Ok, they have two underwater floors of Zeds." I clarified.

"Yes, the base is accessible from underwater. We think that's how they got in. If we clear the two bottom levels and then secure the entries, the base could function again." Rey pointed to the display.

You could see the layout of the bottom-most floor. Toward one side of the base was an entry area. This was made up of a wide central area and three bays that opened from the bottom, like pools. When the base was pressurized, the water would not enter, just like when you held a cup full of air upside down in the tub. Each of these three bays was surrounded by columns that looked like they could be made into separating walls, making sure the bay was discrete. The entire facility, though, was a floating one. And even though it had jets to maintain its position, it wasn't anchored to anything.

"So, we can get in from down here and press upward while they press downward and clear it?"

And your side project got me working on this." Filo put a small device on the table. It looked almost like a taser.

I picked it up, "What is this?"

It's called a screecher. It won't be much help with the human Zeds, but, once I finish it, it will help us clear the rodent and insect ones."

"What happens if I press this?" I really wanted to press the red button.

"go ahead."

I pressed it. Something was happening in the air, a change of some sort. Like pressure. But I couldn't figure out what. "What is that?"

"It's not loud enough yet. But it's a signal, way outside human hearing. If I can get it loud enough it will destroy the nervous systems of Rodents and insects in range." Filo picked it up and placed it proudly back down.

"God Damn." Now I really wanted to push that red button again. But that made me think for a minute. Something had been nagging at me for a while.

I took a breath. "OK. so, second up, what the fuck with a virus that can affect organisms in radically different species. Isn't that odd?" I wasn't sure I wanted to answer that.

Ella switched the holo to an image of the smaller of the two viruses. "It's more than odd. This smaller, virophage, has an incredibly broad host range. And it's vector and consumption- so wet transmission"

"Should we be worried it will branch out and infect, say, a banana?" I asked. I always thought I'd be killed by a banana.

"No. It's apples and oranges, in a way. But honestly, if it did, we should probably just pack it up right then." Ella shrugged.

Behind it, though, I could sense her horror. "If it did find a way to make it to the food supply, we should just go find a new planet."

That actually scared me. "Are we any closer to a cure or vaccine?"

Ella shook her head. I could feel her frustration from across the lab. Maybe if she were back at Port Albert. But after what happened to Dr hull, I wasn't leaving any of my people anywhere.

"Last up, for all the cash, does anyone have any clue what's happening with the time jumps?"

Rey looked around and raised his hand. "It's the only thing I can imagine."

"Ok, spill,"

"These things are built with viruses from the future."

Rivas perked up, "Wait, really?"

I looked over at him. "800 years in the future."

"How is THAT possible?" Rivas looked confused.

I put my hand on his shoulder, "it just gets weirder."

Rey finished, "Is it possible that exposure to these... zeds creates a sort of time-sucking sort of functionality?"

Ella sighed. "Just about anything is possible right now. Literally."

I needed to wrap this up on a high note. "But it's a new reason for us to stay close together. I don't want to lose anyone to the depths of time, either."

***

We arrived on schedule at Duclos Point. The base would be about a kilometer into the water, toward the island, That put it right between where we were and East point Marina. Rey, Rivas, Ella, and Filo stayed in the Lab while I joined Ladia and Symone up on the Nav Pod. Ladia was getting in some hours driving.

I turned to Symone. "OK, your very first task is to connect this screecher immediately to comms channels across the bass and Turn it on. It needs to be on for at least a minute to mulch all the little Zeds. I give you this because I think you understand how vital this is." I made a big Divine sounding presentation noise and handed it to her.

"Hell yes, I do." She held it like it was a sacred idol.

"I have two more of these. Ladia will have one, too. We really can't clear the base without these."

"I will kill them all." Ladia was definitely on board. I felt like Ladia and Symone had bonded completely over their hatred for infected insects. They did sure have a way of creating consensus.

"Filo is using the aggregator to make us all new boots. They will have a metal surface, like the ship's hull.

"Very rock and roll," Ladia interjected.

"Yes, and hopefully good prevention for little nippy things. But they are heavy."

"Got it. Anything else?" Symone reminded me of a world class french waiter, a whole order sitting effortlessly in his mind, waiting for flawless execution.

"No, guys, we just have to pay attention. We don't know what's there.

***

I held onto the third screecher. On my holster, I had a light gun and hanging from my thigh was my crovel. On the back of my neck was a drainer. But what only Filo, Ella, and I knew about was the device on the heel of my left palm.

The killswitch.

To activate it, I needed to reach down with two fingers and press three times. Filo said it required the muscle tension in my hand so only the fingers of that hand could activate it. And it couldn't be activated by anything but my own hand.

I had never been so afraid of my own left hand.

Things were moving quickly. I didn't understand the time shifts, but I was prepared to use them if I needed to.

We approached the root of the base. The ship had to rise about twenty meters to connect and enter the bottom access port. There were three of them, available for swimmers, ships, subs, entryways into the base.

They were all open.

When building the base, they had dug out the lake bed so that it sank far lower than it had. It was nearly twice as deep now as it was years ago when this was just a fun vacation spot. And it was dark. We couldn't see the bottom.

I tried not to think about what was there. Symone tried to use the lower rudder to position the ship so that it rose in the right spot to enter one of the open bays. The Fearless was never designed to float and it only did so because it was full of air we had pressurized. We could use that air to thrust in different directions and the pressure to go up and down. It was no easy effort and the thing made a terrible submarine.

Within a few minutes, though, she had gotten it lined up below a bay and moved upward, lodging the ship into the central one of the three bays. The series of thin columns separating the bays were not expanded, making the room feel open.

Soon, the fearless rose above the bay lid and the tire treads caught, letting it drive up onto the translucent ground of the bay.

The fearless didn't fit perfectly into the area but it fit. We opened the triage bay door and everyone came out slowly, guns drawn. No one was staying inside this time. We were going to stick together for this entire mission, working as a force, if possible, to drive the Zeds off.

I made a motion to Symone and she moved to the comm center toward the far wall. I saw her pull out a screecher and start to connect it to the entire network. Ladia was close behind her. I stayed near the ship and waited for them to get the signal routed. The truth is that we had made a lot of noise. And the base itself was still rumbling, it seemed, from our efforts to climb inside.

At least it seemed that way. I looked at Rey and saw the look on his face. The rumbling increased. If I hadn't been staring right at him, I might have initially missed the cause.

Right behind him, in the first of the bays, a shadow widened, darkening the pool, causing the water to shift and splash over the blue white translucent floors and walls. Suddenly, a massive dark blue tendril rose up out of the water, flailing around the bay space, pulling up the massive body of what looked like a dark blue and white whale. The whale's head emerged into the bay, nearly reaching the roof of the space as its face split down the center vertically, exposing a deep crimson red mouth and a ring of a million metallic teeth. The tendrils kept coming, pulling the monster into the space. The bays began to shift to one side as the bulk of the whale flopped onto the floor, pouring hundreds of gallons of water along with it, leaving about ten centimeters of water all over to trod through.

Rey nearly fell, turning to the Giant sea mammal and letting off a stream of shots from his light gun. It seemed to anger it, even as holes opened up on its surface and the smell of wet rotten cooked meat filled the room.

Symone and Ladia tried to hang on over on the far side of the room, while Ella and Filo climbed to join them. They could see the need to right this and move some bodies over there.

Rivas jumped in shooting the creature with Rey. I raised my gun to take a shot as another shift of the base floor caused me to fall backwards, against the Fearless. I grabbed the jamb of the open door and felt myself start to fall. The ship dipped into the open pool below and fell downward, taking me with it. In that split second, I could have jumped away or held on.

I chose to hold on to the doorway opening, trying to slide inside and close the door, but the ship was falling too fast. I held my breath and felt myself being pulled downward. For a moment I couldn't tell which end was up as it spun laterally falling downward. I crawled to the inside, trying to get into the ship, quickly filling with water, and close the door. I positioned myself over the opening and the ship flipped, inertia from the fall pushing me into the ship.

I felt the thud of the ship hitting the lake bottom, port side down. In panic, I tried to shut the door, but the rocky bottom had invaded the entryway, preventing the door from closing. Water filled the Triage bay, and within seconds it was over my face. I looked upward at the door to the navpod. If I could get in there, I could right this ship. I pushed off.

And realized the metal boots were keeping me firmly planted. I couldn't go anywhere. I was trapped, just a few meters from the door to the NavPod.

The water was dark and cold and for a moment it felt good against the burning sensation in my chest. My lungs were on fire. The urge to take a breath was becoming impossible to ignore. My brain began to compromise, considering the value of just a tiny breath, just a little one. But I knew what would happen.

I was drowning.

I looked at my left hand and considered it. This was untested. But what better time to test it?

I lifted my two middle fingers and pressed the space on my wrist. A wave of red flashed through my head, then black.

I woke up sputtering.

I was still underwater. Nothing had changed.

The killswitch didn't work.

I pressed it again and the same thing happened. I found myself back right when I had pressed it. My loop was too short.

My vision contracted slowly

And I felt myself drown.

12 - Red

I opened my eyes to a glaring light.

I turned to see tendrils invade the docking bay, snaking out from the pool closest to Rey. The floor of the base began to fill with water and dip to my right. For a moment, I could see the Fearless begin to slide through the bay opening. This time I pulled away, grabbing one of the columns surrounding the pool of water.

I could see the Triage bay door open as the ship slid through the pool and out of site.

This time I had decided not to go down with the ship. I realized the time loops were returning me to the decision point that led to my death. If I used the killswitch, that was the deciding point. Otherwise, it was a different one.

It was this one.

I pressed the release on the boots, one at a time, kicking them away, and dove into the pool after the ship. It was descending fast, falling on its starboard side again, where the open door was. The triage bay was filling with water, I guessed, and was heavier and less pressurized than the NavPod, which was discrete. So it would fall with the Navpod door up. I swam harder.

We needed this ship to get off the base, sooner than later, and I wasn't going to let it sit at the bottom of the Simcoe. It was descending faster than me now, but I could see the Navpod door. As soon as it stopped, I would open the Navpod door and fall into it, shutting it as fast as possible.

I could pump the water out and use the jets to lift it just enough to electronically shut the Triage bay doors.

Then pump that water out.

I could be back in the base in less than two minutes if I did this right.

The dark started to waft around me. The water was cold down here, as I remembered. But I was losing time swimming downward, time I didn't have. The ship kept descending, putting me just frustratingly close but too far from the navpod door.

My chest started to feel on fire. It burned and sank under the pressure. My ribs felt as though they might bend and my head began to hurt, building toward a dark brown, red, and then black.

My mouth opened. I took an unintentional breath and poured hot lava into my lungs.

I screamed and died.

***

It was brutally light as I opened my eyes. I leaned against a column and felt for the release for my boots. I took each one and lifted them to my waist. They were heavy and cold.

I barely saw the tendrils rip from the water but my eyes followed the ship slide into the bay pool and sink from sight. I took a deep breath, held tightly to the boots and jumped in, feet first.

I tried to not move, conserving my air and energy. I descended at nearly the same speed as the Fearless, my feet only about three meters from the Navpod door. I pointed my toes and tried to slide into the wake of the ship.

As it got darker, I slowly let the air out of my lungs, one brief puff at a time, Each one thinning the air in my lungs, preventing the pressure in the water outside from crushing me.

I felt the water shift as the ship hit the bottom. I could barely see but my toes touched the door about two seconds after. I kept hold of the boots and sank, pressing my palm up against the NavPod door and falling in as it slid open. I fell backward into the NavPod and slammed my hand against the door close. The space was only about a third filled with water. I took a deep breath and let it out, holding tightly to the seat.

Reaching for a button in front of me, I started pumping the water out of navigation. The air that filled the space came in hot, drying the control area in front of me and causing the droplets accumulating on the monitors to dissipate. I hit the starboard side thruster and it lifted the ship just about ten centimeters, enough to order the Triage Bay door shut.

I started a timer as the water was pumped from the Triage Zone. I was using too much energy to lift the ship, but I didn't care. We could charge it back up later, once we were on dry land.

The ship started rising. My timer read 1:34 as I tried to mentally add how long it had taken me to descend.

The front monitors sprung to life and I could see the bay above me. Flailing in the far bay, I could see the Infected whale, shaking and causing the entire base to tilt.

The Fearless didn't have too much in the way of weaponry, but it did have guns at front and specimen collection tanks that could be fired with significant force. I banked the ship toward the Whale trying to get its attention with two specimen tanks, torpedoes that slid through the water and slammed through the whale's rotting flesh, One directly through its underside, lodging in its belly.

The whale slid down, angry, moving faster than I thought possible for something so large, and moved toward me. Its face opened vertically as it prepared to extricate me from the ship with its ring of massive metallic teeth.

I primed every gun, remembering what we had seen in the forest on the way to Tobermory.

I began firing everything I had right into the center of its massive red maw. I saw the blackness of its throat open and blood pour out. It shook and flailed while I kept shooting until there wasn't a single bullet left in the ship. The meat from the whale spun around its center mass, as the bloody water trail widened.

Anything swimming through that would be infected.

I pointed the ship up at the bay. Hitting the thrusters hard this time. It rose up over the floor and I could feel the tire treads catch on the translucent floor space in front of me.

I climbed out. Rey was the first to meet me at the NavPod doorway.

"That was novel."

"It took me a couple of tries to figure it out." I turned, "Rivas, Filo, Can you close these bays hard? There may soon be a lot of infected shit swimming around. I could see the water splashing onto the base floor running pink now. Soon all the water surrounding the base would be blood red and infected.

But I had no choice. That was the only choice that led to some kind of success.

Rey and I made our way to the com area. Ladia and Symone had started the screecher broadcast. Ella ran over to me to check me out.

"I'm fine, Bel."

"Did you die?"

"I did."

"How many times?"

"I think, a few. The killswitch doesn't work. I mean it works great, but…"

"We'll figure it out. You need new boots."

By the time we got back out of the Fearless with a new set of boots and a couple more guns, everyone was collected around the Starboard Triage Bay doors.

Rey looked at me, "ok, All entrances are battened down, no way in. Screechers are on and transmitting across the whole base. All doorways into the base from here are locked down too, so we can plan. Everyone is ready but we've had no contact yet with the base complement."

"Yes, we have." Rivas shouted. He held up his phone where he'd managed to connect with his fiancé, Daanis. "Are you still there?"

"Yes, sweetheart, we're all here. We're all on the top floor." Her voice sounded scared but resolute.

I leaned into his phone. "Lieutenant Eagle, hi, this is Colonel Pinga of the Fearless. How many of you are there and is everyone ok?"

My voice seemed to snap her back into a matter of fact business space. "Hello, Colonel. We have twenty people left and the north half of the top floor secured. - ten rooms out of fifteen."

"Good work. Do you have any big injuries or wounds on your team?"

We waited what seemed like a full minute for her to respond. I looked at Filo with his bag of drainers but I knew that if someone had been already bitten it would probably be no good. We didn't really know enough.

"No. All in good shape, Colonel."

"I love you, Daanis," Rivas wasn't going to miss the opportunity.

"I love you, too."

"And we all love you, good work keeping those people alive. Can you keep this line open?"

"We love you." Ladia yelled out.

Rivas nodded and moved away to talk to his wife.

"When you die, do you leave little ghosts everywhere?"

I looked over at Ladia. I knew this was her way of dealing with weird shit. "I wish. I'd literally haunt the fuck out of you, bitch."

"Bring it, Casper." She stepped over toward me slowly, "I really hate these boots."

"They're good for some things. But, I'll tell you what. If we can run these screechers for a while, I'll stop worrying about crawly things that bite and you can trade them in for some uggs."

"Sweet. I like it." Ladia slammed her foot down. "Seriously, though, did that suck?"

On one level, yes, it sucked, I thought. But I'm alive. And so was everyone else. "I need to figure this time shit out. Maybe we can use it positively."

"Alright, I think that's enough cycles." Symone stepped over to us, "I think everything rodent or insect is dead."

"Fucking spiderman and the easter bunny begone." Ladia waved her hand.

"Ok, let's see what everything else looks like."

**

The holo of the rest of this level wasn't hopeful looking. There were about fifteen rooms on this floor and ten of them were flooded. According to the internal sensors, the five that were still air-filled contained three human sized Zeds. The remaining water filled space, however, contained one.

Something massive

"Can you tell what that is," I pointed, squinting at the Holo.

"No idea," Filo tried to adjust the sensors.

Rey cocked his head "I've never seen that shape."

"It's like a giant broccoli" Ladia

Ella shook her head, "that would be game over. I'm serious. If this thing's starting to infect actual food, we're screwed."

"Ok, so it's not a broccoli. We'll find out soon enough." I put my hand on her shoulder. "We need rebreathers. Anything else?"

"Some hand held pumps that can move us through the water." Rey offered.

"I can do that," Filo was keeping track in his head.

I leaned against the comm station and looked around as Filo, Ella and Rey returned to the Fearless to get what we needed. The base was impressive but not larger than it needed to be. The walls were translucent, glowing in blues and whites on three sides. The floor below us was nearly clear, rippling with the tensions of the water just beyond it. There were still swirls of red, like tiered smoke collecting around an offering, pale pink waste from the ruined infected whale. I couldn't help but think of the entire lake as infected, full of this strange futuristic pox that carried living genes like tiny spaceships built for a more brutal time.

I looked down at the tiny rise of the killswitch in my palm. It seemed terrifying for something that had proven so pointless. It had no power to send me anywhere but back to the point right before i'd pushed it. It was my choices, my decisions, that were driving this weird temporal loop. I thought about how my choices here could kill other people permanently while allowing me to rise again, untouched, to decide again.

How could that help Herman, trapped in the back of that plane while I struggled to keep it from killing more people? The truth is, it couldn't. Herman was gone and no futuristic time virus was going to fix that. He was a good man. How many other good people were going to die because of this insane war, and, more proximally, my choices as I tried to fight it?

I stepped around the comm desk and moved in the direction of the Fearless. All of this thinking about the past had put me into a state I didn't need to be in during a mission. I tried to shake it off. Ladia walked over and stood next to me.

She pointed off to the right.

At first I thought someone from our team had moved away from the ship and was standing there. The shape was in silhouette against the light blue white wall, glowing with its own light. As soon as my eyes adjusted, I saw it was a man. He was just finishing stripping off the last of his clothes. I could see the trail of clothing, bloody, wet, torn, leading from an open door to the rest of the facility and where he was standing. He was facing the wall, with his back to us, trying to look out into the water.

"It's ok. I know you're there." His voice cracked emotionally.

"Who are you," I raised my light gun.

"It got in my mouth. I only have a minute or so." He spit on the ground.

I turned to Ladia, "Quick, grab a drainer."

"It's no use." He turned to us. He was fully naked now. "I can feel the change."

"We can stop it. "

"No, you can't."

Rey and Symone appeared to my left, guns drawn. "Are you ok?" Rey asked, keeping his eyes locked on the figure. I nodded.

"This is for the record, ok?" He was tall, maybe six foot, lightly tanned, caucasian, short cropped black hair. His breathing was already heavy. He was covered in sweat. "I feel strong. Like my body is fixing itself. I feel muscular and… my reflexes."

"You need to put one of these on," I moved toward him, holding a drainer that Rey had given me.

"No, No, No. Stay away. You're not listening to me. You have to record it. And keep your guns on me."

"This can stop it." I put it on the floor and kicked it over to him. He seemed angry, unstable.

"My heart is beating. So fast. There's, like, an anger here. It's so big. If I let it…It would kill me just to kill you."

Rey tried to catch his attention. "Don't let go. Put that on. Put it on right now, soldier."

"I'M NOT A SOLDIER. I'm not anything anymore." He dropped down onto his knees. He started crawling. He patted his hands around the floor. I could see his limbs beginning to elongate, stretching, cracking, breaking. The spinal hump in the back of his neck rose in an unwieldy arch. He continued to talk in a passionless, professional way, capturing his transition in an oral soliloquy, like a forensic scientist speaking into a recorder, as he crawled toward his clothing. "The elongation of the limbs feels like bones breaking, on fire, ripping and reforming the muscles. The pain is amazing. It's inspiring."

His voice was like a visiting lecturer at some bizarre college. He crawled forward.

He looked up. His breath was coming faster. Ella and Filo had come out and we all stood there, surrounding him. I looked down at the drainer sitting uselessly on the ground.

"What's your name… For the record?"

He crawled to his gun in jerky accelerated movements. His voice dropped. If I closed my eyes I could imagine him sitting sanely across a college lab table, a pointer in his hand. There was pain there, but it was buried.

Deep down.

"I don't have a name. I don't feel like an I anymore. There is a hurricane in me, an ageless one. It doesn't need a name. It's everything. It's every name."

He let out a low groan. "I can feel you move from here. The hurricane lets me feel the wind. I can sense the movement of your hair." His arms snapped backward, eliciting quick grunts.

"Don't touch that gun, son." Rey said slowly.

"Gun, son." He laughed loudly. The laugh wrapped around the room, resonating against the glassine glow of the walls, resolving into a growl that sounded familiar. "I want."

I imagined his brain dissolving. The frontmost part turning to gel, slowly leaking backward and down, making way for the massive ring of metallic teeth lurking just behind the skin of his face. I raised my gun, and squinted, scanning his eyes for humanity. This presentation, all of it, it seemed like a game now.

"How many are in there still?" I tried to be casual. To keep him talking.

"Of us. How many of us. There are three more of us, but there are millions if you look right." He pointed his head at me, "You could see. You are real."

"Wait, what do you mean, she is real?" Ladia took a step closer to him and I grabbed her arm. The last thing I needed was to lose someone right now.

"She is part of the wave. The wave that moves forward." He began to shake and a stream of blood shot out of his mouth across the floor. He vibrated more quickly and looked up at us. His arm reached forward and I saw him palm his gun. Symone called out. I lifted my light gun as his face opened, a dark red slit down the center. Blood poured from his mouth as he launched himself toward us. I lifted my gun and severed his arm as Ladia shot directly into his face.

We all backed off as he screamed, hit from all sides with coherent light rays and bullets. Rey removed his head with a final shot and the momentum sent it spinning across the room.

I saw motion across my entire periphery and I tried to back away to take it all in. His body convulsed then fell still. I breathed in and quickly surveyed the room.

To the right of Rey I could see that Filo had stepped in front of Ella to protect her. He stood there, breathing heavily.

His face and mouth were covered in blood.

13 - Aqua

One of the things that is standard in every Zombie movie, a trope, even, is that no one finds a cure. People become so immersed in killing zombies, so invested in protecting the people left behind, so anxious to get a moment of clarity, of rest, of respite, that they fail to even search for one.

They die without a solution - without a cure.

We blocked off the doors and assembled in the fearless. This wasn't going to happen to us. We were going to find a cure.

We were going to find a solution.

"How do you feel," Rey hovered over Filo as he stepped out of the clean room. He'd been scrubbed down sonically. Without a shirt on you could see the drainer on the back of his neck. I gave silent thanks for that.

"I'm infected. I can feel it. There's a kind of battle going on inside me. I feel different. It's not advancing but I can feel it."

Ella was leaning against the lab table with her head down. I lifted up her head. "We're going to find a cure. YOU'RE going to find a cure. You have to."

She nodded, her face, covered in tears, "He was trying to protect me."

"I was just doing my job. This isn't anyone's fault." He looked over at her. I could tell he was afraid to get close.

"I get it. I do." I nodded at Rey. He followed me into the NavPod where Rivas was keeping watch on the bass from the monitors.

"Any updates?" Rey asked, trying to leave the other room behind him.

Rivas shook his head. "No changes. The door is holding. I can't help but feel this is all my fault."

"Exactly none of it is your fault, Rivas. Here. I'll relieve you here. Why don't you go back to the lab and get checked out, quickly, then we can take two breaths and get back to the job."

"Yes sir, Colonel." He stepped through the door and into the Lab.

I looked over at Rey. "Ok, spill. What are you thinking?"

He sighed, "I'm not really thinking right now. I wish I had some kind of rewind here. Is there a way to, you know, fix this?"

"Can I die and undo it?"

"I don't know what I'm thinking. I'm sorry."

"No, it's fair. I tried to figure it out, too. I would need a particular decision to kill me, and,,,"

"Yes, I don't know what we could have done. We need to wear masks all the time moving forward."

"Agreed. This thing is more highly infectious than we initially thought. We need to prevent all body fluid transmission until we find a cure."

"Do you really think we will? This virus is eight hundred years more advanced than that lab in there."

"We'll find it because we have to. And Ella's good. Before she was in the field, she did a lot of pure research work. She was kind of a savant when we were kids."

"That's right, you grew up with her and Lieutenant Arrakis."

"Ha. Yes. Ella and I were always close. It wasn't until we joined up, though, that Ladia and I got to be good friends. Ella brought us together. She forced us to stop fighting."

"Funny how that works sometimes. The person in between."

"I know Filo is important to you?"

"Finn? Yes. I admit I'm a bit of a wreck right now. "

"He defected to you?"

"Yes, technically he is a citizen of the United Nations now. He was part of the American resistance almost from the first day. He and his brother stole over the border and came to me. He was just a kid, really."

"And you made it happen."

"He has a good heart. It's funny because I probably would have tossed his brother Manny out of the starboard bay without him."

I laughed, "Yep, he's a force, huh?"

"Manny is the leader. Filo is the diplomat."

"Plus he's a fucking genius."

"There is that." Rey sat for a second, "I need him to be ok."

I turned to Rey and looked him right in the eye. "Me, too, Rey. I need that, too."

Rey nodded. "So, are we going to hug now?"

"Nope. I've made the mistake before of trying to hug one of you British people. Let's gather up and do this."

***

In my head, I was starting to call the little time jumps triggered by my death "slips." And there was a lot in them to explore. Through these slips I was steadily beginning to discover what didn't work. It wasn't perfect and it was painful as hell, but it was my advantage. Maybe the only real one I had.

I was assembling a list in my head of things I wanted made, based on some of my slips. The boots were helpful for walking around here before we were able to set the screecher. But even more helpful as a weight when I needed to descend into the water quickly. Maybe a device that we could use in the water to rapidly ascend or descend. Rebreathers would let us breathe underwater and also keep infected liquids from getting in our mouths. And we should all be carrying a light gun. These futuristic guns were hard to figure out but they were far more effective with these monsters.

Filo managed to get all of these output by the aggregator. And twenty five minutes later, we were all in the Triage Bay Zone with him explaining them.

"Ok, guys. These rebreathers will filter and cycle oxygen from the water. The facial covering is meant to prevent anything from getting in your mouth or eyes. It won't fog up so if you can't see, don't take it off, it's not the rebreather's fault."

Ladia already had hers on, "Good to know."

"Oh, and Rey, you can't wear your contacts in it, because of the pressure differentials, so yours is based on your prescription lens." Ella handed a special one to Rey.

"Thank you."

I realized I didn't even know that he needed contacts. Filo and Ella had learned so much about all these people. Not for the first time I found myself so proud of her.

"These are light guns for everyone. They will work underwater, but even coherent light is refracted by water, so watch where you shoot."

He passed out the pistols while Ella picked up two large light gun rifles and gave them to Ladia and Symone.

"We were able to make a couple upgraded ones. They have a serious kick. We really don't know how that will translate in the water, so…"

Ladia looked at Symone and mouthed her approval. She seemed to enjoy the heft of it. Symone looked through the sights. "This is amazing."

"This is so fucking Tron." Ladia loved it.

Filo smiled. "And lastly, these are waterdrives." Ella handed out devices that clipped to our belts about the size and shape of a beer can. "You squeeze them to activate. Keep the open area behind you, that's the jet. It pulls in water through the permeable area in front. So keep your hands away from both sides. In the air, it probably makes a nice fan."

Ella and Filo looked around the room. She took a breath.

"Any Questions?"

***

We moved through the door and into the adjoining room. Beyond the next door would be the first of the Zeds we would need to eliminate. I took point and the other six stepped through two by two. This was going to be our formation through these rooms. It gave everyone less than 180 degrees of space to be vigilant about and kept us together.

This space was a lab. It was torn apart and looked as though it had been ravaged. As I looked around, I could see it was filled with evidence that the screechers had done their jobs. Small rodents and large insects littered the floor, exploded like small balloons of blood against the antiseptic space of a lab that was clearly state of the art at one point, despite the fact that it looked more like an old storage space now.

I advanced to the doorway in front of me. It was wide, more like a garage door than anything. The room was dark but the array of small lights on the comm system on the wall suggested that the door might still open. It looked like it would open from the far end toward us.

I turned to the team and nodded. I leaned into the release and for a moment, it looked like the door would slide open as quickly and smoothly as all these doors had. Instead, It shot open for the first ten centimeters or so and then stopped, seemingly jammed.

I looked back and Filo shrugged. "These are internally seated. There must be some damage to this wall in the other room."

"Shit." It was clear we weren't going to fit. And we didn't really have the opportunity to play around. Our sensors said there was a Zed in there and part of me felt like this particular one was mine. I pressed the button again and it slid shut. One more time delivered the exact same results the first time had.

I had taken a step toward the opening when I heard the scream from the other room, followed by a series of sounds, objects falling, scrambling. It sounded like a rugby match, coordinated feet, but blind, frenetic, mad. The room shook as the monster slammed into the wall, trying to drive itself through to our side. Its head slid through the opening, tentacles reaching outward, leaving bloody tracks on our side of the door and the far wall. Its head wrenched its way through the slot between the door and wall and screamed, opening up like a gash vertically down the center of its once-human face.

I saw the ring of silver, sharpened teeth and imagined I could feel the air pumping from its misshapen, altered lungs, pouring out of its red, inflamed mouth, even through the rebreather. Infected blood gushed from its open mouth, forcing all of us to pull back and Rivas to fall over, advancing backward, to the floor where he pulled himself away from the monster like a crab, trying his best to avoid the bloodied stains on the floor. .

Ladia reached over and pulled him out, giving me time to respond, quickly.

I lifted my light gun and fired directly into his torn open face, above the mouth, trying to obliterate the brain. Symone did as well. He squealed and his head shot back, the stench of boiling rotten meat invading the room, past the polyglass masks we wore.

Until the world exploded.

For a split second, it looked like the monster itself erupted into living flame, bursting outward and ripping through the floor below him and the wall itself. Tentacles exploded outward as though he were growing huge, sending pieces of the beast everywhere. As the floor beneath me gave way, I realized that there had been something behind it in that room, something that had detonated under the energy surges of the light guns. I tried to turn to look at the others but my feet slid through the hole beneath me as the roof came crashing down, propelling me downward.

The water was full of blood and debris, much of it from the space above us, which was completely filled with water and garbage. I made a mental note of that and let myself be carried downward. The explosion had pushed me northward, away from the base. I was falling on an angle, already too far from where I had started to comfortably swim back.

I made sure my rebreather was tight and reached for the waterdrive at my waist. I didn't like being so far away from the team. But I was. I had no visibility. No sign of any of them.

The explosion had seriously damaged the base. It didn't escape my understanding here that my best bet was to let myself die and timeslip back to try that again. I could easily kill that single Zed with a crovel, avoiding the lightshow, and I made a mental note to think of that as the first line of attack from now on. The problem is that I didn't really understand these timeslips and had no clue when they would stop.

My instinct was still not to rush to die.

It occured to me, as well, that I had descended farther than I should have been able to given the depth of this lake. Even with the work that had been done to build the base, digging down on the lake bed to lower the floor, I should have slammed into the bottom already.

Over toward the south a bit, when I fell through with the Fearless, we had hit the lake bed long before this.

I tried to take in everything I could. These moments where I was due to die momentarily only served me if I could remember everything I possibly could. I estimated from the pressure that i must have been about 60 meters down, considering, for a moment, how fucked up it was that I was now getting so used to drowning that I could gauge the crushing pressure. The big problem with that was that Lake Simcoe didn't go 60 meters down. I pushed off from the wall of debris above me, hoping to escape it moving downward.

The waterdrive propelled me down and away from the pieces of flooring. It felt like moving through gel as I lifted my hand to turn on the light in my rebreather. The pressure was starting to feel oppressive. It took significant effort to breathe in and I felt the limits my lungs could expand to, as though they were shrinking.

I kept my eyes open as long as I could as I descended, falling further. I had reached the point at which my lungs wouldn't inflate anymore. It must have been over a hundred meters down. Looking down, the hole beneath me seemed endless. As my vision darkened, I wondered if i would really snap back this time.

And why there was a hole in a tiny Canadian lake that went down literally hundreds of meters.

***

I opened my eyes to a shock of light and the screech of the Zed, his head trapped in the half-open doorway. I turned to Symone and pressed my hand on her rifle, lowering it. I shook my head and pulled out my crovel. Rey broke ranks and met me, his own crovel extended, as we ripped open the monster's head.

With the rebreathers, we were covered head to toe, but I still flinched, backing away from the spray of blood from the infected thing as it died, furiously expelling liquids across the lab.

I waited until the room was quiet. "Ok, something in that room is seriously explosive. Let's be careful until we clear it.

Ladia understood right away, "What else did you learn?"

"The room above us is filled with water and junk. And there is a massive open crater down there slightly to the north. Oh, and the water is real cold.

Rivas looked around the room. "Ok, what am I missing here?"

Rey stepped forward, "When she gets killed, she goes a little bit back in time and comes back to life."

"I'm going to pretend I understand what you're talking about."

"It's like in a movie where someone relives the same thing over and over." Ella tried to be helpful.

Rivas was having a lot of trouble processing, "So, you know how all this ends?"

I shook my head, "no. but if I try something and it ends up killing me, I can snap back and sometimes try something different. This is why I'm taking point from now on."

"Is this connected to the the time issue we had?" He was trying to make sense of it.

Filo jumped in, "We think so, but it's all kind of unknown right now."

Rey was peering into the space beyond the doorway.

"Well, this room seems empty now. If we can jimmy this door open a bit more, we can get to the others." We worked together to pull the door back far enough to enter the room.

"Is this it?" I asked Filo, standing in front of a row of about 30 clear cylinders filled with translucent blue liquid.

"Yep. Fuel. A lot of it. My guess is that this bass can function as a refueling station, with ships entering through the side bay ports we came from and fueling up. There's enough here for…. Well, a lot."

"Well, let's make sure we point all guns away from it. In my slip, this took out much of this floor and the one above us." I looked at him. He seemed ok.

"How are you feeling?"

He breathed out, leaning against the lab table. "I feel good. I feel under control. It's just a thing in the back of my head right now. But we're going to find a cure."

Ella pulled up next to us and put her hand over his. "We are. We're going to find a cure."

"I would listen to her. She's not messing around." I tried to sound optimistic and confident, even though I was feeling neither right now. But I knew what I had to be.

"Excuse me, Colonel." Rivas had come up behind me.

"Tomi is fine. What's up?"

"Well, Daanis says they have the top level cleared. Once we get this level and the one above, we can meet up there. But she says they lost contact."

"With Port Albert?"

"Um, with everyone. With all the other bases. She says that we are the only contact they have."

"That can't be right." I motioned to Rey, who stepped over. "Rivas says that the people here lost all contact with other bases."

Rey looked down at the communicator in his hand. "That seems about right."

"Do we have anything? Canadian Military, UN? Anything?" I looked into his face.

"No. Nothing. I keep thinking they'll come back online, but I don't have anything."

"Wait, do you have satellites? Can we link?"

"That's something I was going to talk to you about once this was done."

"I don't like the sound of that. Rey, what is it?"

He looked over at Filo. He shook his head. "I managed to connect to a climatology satellite. I have no human presence, but it is transmitting a status message, with weather, date, and other details." He called up the transmission and showed me the communicator.

"Minor storms. No big deal."

"Keep reading." Rey pointed it at my face.

The date was 200 years in the future.

14 - Bleed

"When were you going to tell us this?" I'd known her long enough to know that the anger was something that happened when Ladia was trying not to let her fear show through.

"Rey was right. Either we work through these monsters and clear the base or we sit around a table and try to figure out when time has gone psychotic on us. Trying to do both is only going to get us killed." I gave her a look that she should have recognized by now.

"Ok, ok, fair. What do we do now?"

I sighed, "it wouldn't make sense to have more cylinders of fuel scattered all over in every room, would it?"

Filo shook his head, "No. That's the storage area, I'm betting."

"Great. Let's still try to avoid putting any holes in this thing." I turned to Rivas, "How is everyone upstairs?"

He looked like he was maybe a bit more put together now. I could tell that his fiance's welfare was burning brightly in his mind. "Good. They are laying low down on the top floor, waiting for us."

"Good. That's where they need to stay, all together." Rey had no interest in herding other people's cats, even as we all tried to stick together.

And I agreed with him 100%..

"That's right. We're going to be there as fast as we can. This mission is to make sure this base is secure and tight."

Rivas nodded. All of this was what he needed to hear. He needed to feel powerful - that he was keeping them safe. He was far better at managing his concern for his own safety than his fear for hers. That I got.

"Ok, Colonel, the other two small ones are behind that door there. Past that room it's submerged and our big bogie is moving around in a pretty big space. The water filled area. It's about a third of the station size, maybe a thousand square meters." Filo had conjured a holo from a small black plate he had brought with.

Ladia tried to shift the holo around. "No way to see that thing better?" She stared at it. It still looked to be the general shape of a broccoli.

No, I'm using heat. Which brings up an important point. Living things, like us, generate heat. Full blown zeds generate a LOT of heat, like a furnace. But organisms in transition, they are technically dead. And they are flat."

"Flat?" I looked over at Filo.

He shrugged apologetically. "Room temperature."

Elle jumped in, "That must be how we missed that guy transitioning."

"He was dead?" Rivas looked confused. "He was talking and moving."

"Yeah. all of this is a mystery. I think we need to table some of them." I motioned toward the door. "Everyone ready to go through that?"

***

"I wish we knew which ones of these had drainers on them. A long distance poison gas solution makes sense." Filo was thinking as we moved in formation past the door and into the wide open room beyond. It was dark and cold and powerless, looking dead. In the center of the room it looked as though all the furniture and equipment had been piled up, in some attempt to blockade those thighs.

Symone nodded, "I like that idea. I want to kill all of them from far away." There was a chill in her voice that seemed appropriate.

I admit that I liked the idea, too. This was on the agenda, I thought, "Let's keep our eyes open. If anyone sees a drainer on these monsters, yell out."

Suddenly, Filo broke formation. He ran forward, pulling at the blockade, tearing it down. I could hear the sounds from beyond it. Those things were behind the wall of junk.

"Filo!" Rey ran forward, the rest of us moving to keep up. I caught up to Filo, pulling a desk down from the pile in between us and the monsters. "What are you thinking?"

He was sweating. I could feel the fever coming off him. Being here, so close to those things, was affecting him. "We can't let them break through. It's worse together."

Ella grabbed his arm, "What are you talking about?"

"I can feel it. They're trying to connect." Filo rested his hand casually on her waist. "We can't let them."

I started attacking the blockade. We all pulled it apart in pieces. The space beyond it was like a cave, and the lights from our rebreathers couldn't penetrate. We could hear the Zeds beyond but they weren't charging at us. They were occupied doing something else. I pushed Filo aside and launched myself into the hole we had ripped from the blockade. I could see movement on the other side of the room. Just as we had been tearing at the blockade of gear and furniture, the two zeds across the room had been tearing at the far wall.

Beyond it was water. And that thing.

The wall they were trying to tear through was a communications center, covered in monitors. They had ripped them down and were digging through the thick cement behind them. Their motions could be described as fanatical, passionate, almost uncontrollable as they tore at the wall with their hands, mouths, and the tendrils extending off of them. I fired at one of them, a direct shot through the back of its head and another through its shoulder. It barely slowed down. I pulled out my projectile gun and began to shoot, carving off pieces of each.

Ladia was right beside me shooting. She managed to neatly score the neck of one of them, nearly severing its head. As we approached behind it, she lifted her crovel and dug into the root of its neck, removing the head completely. It fell to the ground with tendrils outstretched and began to move, ratlike, toward her as she fired into its open maw, destroying the scurrying head.

The body seemed to stop and slide down the wall, giving the illusion that this was only a minor pause- a temporary cessation in its drive to power through the wall.

The other slammed its head into the wall again and again, spraying blood all around like the backlash of a garden hose half covered by fingers. We pulled back, avoiding the poisoned blood, except for Filo who let out a howl and slammed a sharpened pole into the back of the monster.

One final impact of the beast's head into the wall broke through, creating an indent in the wall thin enough for water from the other side to dig its way through. It began slowly and then slammed through like a jackhammer, sending water pouring into the room we were in.

I tried to keep my balance and considered the endgame here for a moment. This floor was underwater and could take on water completely if not sufficiently pressurized. I wasn't sure if the hole on the other side of that far room was still open or not.

Best case, we were about to be chest deep in water.

Worst case, completely underwater with infected lake pouring in. And by my estimates we wouldn't find out for at least two more minutes.

I tried to track everyone in the group. Ladia and Symone were right by me. Rey and Ella were flanking Filo about four meters to my left.

I didn't see Rivas.

"Rivas! Call out. Rivas."

No answer. For a second i thought I heard Filo call out something but it was too late. I was underwater swimming toward the far room. I reached down to the waterdrive at my waist and used it to propel me through the hole. Out of the corner of my eye I could see Ladia right behind me as I tried to catch up to Rivas, who was being dragged through the hole by the remaining monster.

I grabbed at his leg and he tried to reach for me. I pulled backward as Ladia shot erratically toward the Zed underwater. The current became wild with the heat of the gun and I could see a light shot rip through the beast's right shoulder, cleaning severing its arm. I pulled Rivas back and reversed the waterdrive, yanking the arm out.

I tried to stand, pulling Rivas up with me until his head was above water. I quickly checked his rebreather.

It was in one piece.

Ladia rose up from the water about two meters to my right. The water was at the level of our chests and not rising.

It looked like the integrity of the far room was in place. Rivas looked at me, nodding. I waited until he had pulled his gun up and let go of him, stepping back toward Ladia. Symone moved up right behind us.

"Is everyone ok?"

Filo called out, "I can feel that thing. It's here."

My eyes were starting to become accustomed to the dim light in this room and the waves of water were dying down, leaving us in a thousand square meter room, covered in about a meter and a half of murky poisoned water.

But no monster.

"I don't see it. Does anyone have eyes on it?"

It was still too dark. But it was possible to see a massive shape under the water. At first, it just looked like a shadow.

Then a tentacle shot up and fell flat on the surface of the water, slamming down hard, creating a boom that sent waves pulsing across the room, threatening to tip us over.

"And there it is. Some kind of giant fucking squid." Ladia called out.

A second tentacle pulled itself out of the water and reached out, slamming into Rey and throwing him against the wall. Ladia and Symone shot at it, barely making a mark in the dark green limb, ridged with raw, bloody pucker-like shapes and cilia. More than anything, it looked primal, almost prehistoric.

But it wasn't.

I tried to scan the room for Rey and saw him climb up onto a table, out of the water. He used the high ground to start a barrage, attacking the central mass of the monster. It shifted in the water, churning the entire space into a massive whirlpool. A tentacle upended the table and sent him flying as two more reached for our two centralized groups. I pulled my crovel out and dragged a long gash across its arm, unintentionally sending infected blood across the room.

Grabbing Rivas arm, I pulled back toward the far wall. I figured that we were already arrayed in two discrete groups. In order to attack both of us at the same time, it would need to be huge.

How big was it?

The other tentacle slammed into Filo's chest. In a split second it had dug its way through him and pushed him underwater.

I saw Rey dive in after him. Ella began shooting a few meters upward from the area, hoping to excise that tentacle while Symone and I aimed for the main mass of the creature.

The water dropped at least ten centimeters across the room as the head of the massive Zed lifted up into the air. It was huge. It looked like some kids' party Octopus mold of green and red jello, slick and filled with dark indecipherable shapes. Its face rose up and split wide open, from top to bottom, revealing a round ring of metal-clad teeth, each as long as my forearm, while infected blood pulsed from its throat, a blackish red hole in the center of its face, spitting and birthing brackish ropes that seemed to slither on their own, prowling the surface of the water.

It lifted two tentacles above the water. Impaled on one of them was the Zombie that had grabbed Rivas, kicking and growling, its own mouth wide and pulsing, ring of teeth visible in the dark by dint of reflection from the dimming lights of our rebreathers.

And on the other, the form of Filo, a tentacle emerging from his chest, holding him aloft over the surface of the water. He was frantically trying to release himself. We fired on the tentacle, trying to sever it while Rey advanced, hoping to pull him off. His face was contorted. I moved closer, trying to look for the tiny metallic glint of the drainer on the back of his neck, but I couldn't see anything.

He screamed.

"What do we do," Symone had been aiming into the mouth of the giant creature but it seemed to be taking no real damage.

I turned to her. "We need to be giving Rey an opening to get him down. No time."

Ladia, Symone and Rivas tried to get its attention, pumping as much ordinance as possible into the wide open flaps of its mouth. It reached down and shifted the tentacles across its left axis and slammed a wall of water into us. It hit like a bus.

"Rey, can you reach him?"

Ella was covering him, but Rey was still unable to extricate Filo from the Tentacle. His screams were filling the space, pouring out over the top of the water until they suddenly stopped.

He hung there, as if dead. And then, he started speaking, low at first, in a guttural growl that seemed to come from the bottom of the ocean.

"OFFER YOU THE CHANCE TO LEAVE."

I looked back and forth. Ella was frantically scanning the beast for a place to shoot. For a way to do anything.

"Let him go. If you let him go, we'll leave." I lied, advancing closer.

"THERE IS NO HIM. NOTHING TO LET GO OF."

"Put his body down and move away and we'll leave."

"SAME BODY." Filo's mouth spat the words out. On the other side of the room, the tentacle holding the zombie swung toward us. From the creature's open maw came a mangled version of the same mantra, "SAME BODY."

Filo repeated, "SAME BODY."

"We're not leaving without him." I asserted.

"Put him down," Rey lifted his gun again.

"We don't want to have to hurt you." I tried to sound reassuring.

The tentacles rose higher. Filo's eyes looked around the room. For a moment, it seemed like he was back - that he was in there. He inhaled and sputtered. Then, as if coming out of hypnosis, he jerked up, "You have to go,. It wants you to go. It never goes back."

Rey looked up at him, "We're getting you down."

"You have to go..."

Out of the corner of my eye, I saw Ladia break ranks and move away toward the side of the creature. She was moving slowly so as not to disturb the water. I tried to occupy it to give her a chance.

"Tell it to let you go. We'll get out of here. It can have the whole base."

"Colonel, I'm sorry."

"It's ok, let's just get out of here, ok," Part of me hoped that the connection he had with this thing could convince it. I couldn't see any other way. But I could see him changing. There was no sign of the drainer.

We had no time.

Ella climbed up on a table and reached for him. I could see him trying to pull himself from off the tentacle as he extended himself toward her. Rey placed himself under the tentacle. I realized something while watching him prepare to shoot through the appendage.

This thing was looking at me. It was focused on me.

There were seven of us, but, for some reason, I was the one it was primarily addressing.

I yelled out, "Hey. Are we done? Don't you want to negotiate? Do you want us gone?"

The other tentacle carrying the zombie swung toward me. The creature spat out, "NO DEAL. JUST GONE."

It wanted to be alone more than it wanted to fight us. I looked at Rey and nodded. I lifted my light gun and drilled into the mouth of the monster. The larger creature screamed and pulled back, while Rey shot, severing the tentacle holding Filo. Ella pulled him off of it and the two of them fell hard against the tables arrayed against the wall to my left.

Far to my right, Ladia Dropped onto the top of the creature's uppermost tentacle. She had climbed a pipe leading up the far wall and now worked her way to the massive squid-creature's mouth.

She had wrapped something around a water drive, tying it to her light rifle. She dug it live and pulsing into the raw red mouth of the monster and pushed down, letting the drive catch on the liquid blood spew and accelerate. All at once, the inside of the thing lit up as though it were an ornament from some demented christmas tree. It flailed, sending water slamming into the walls of the room, upending us. The whine of the light rifle intensified.

"Ladia!" I moved forward as fast as i could trying to reach her. The squid-like Zed spread its tentacles blindly around the room and we could see the full size of it. There were dozens of tentacles, each as long and thick as a fully grown tree, powerful, rapacious, unrelenting.

I could hear the light rifle overload, the screeching whine getting louder by the second, stuck in the massive animal's neck until finally, the creature's head exploded. It was impossibly loud, the death knell of the light rifle, pulling into it the flash of the infected squid's entire head. That death message hadn't yet reached the tentacles, which still lashed out frenetically, faster than their size would seem to allow. My ears seemed to invert and suddenly the world was muted, a pillow over my head.

I heard nothing, even thoughl was less than ten meters from Ladia as two massive green stems ripped her body at the waist into two pieces, throwing the parts against the far wall with enough force to nearly liquefy them.

I screamed soundlessly and fired into the pulsing morass of the monster again and again. The water around us was nothing but blood now, this massive bleed pushing all life aside like an artery dispensing with bacteria, flushing out the system striving for some kind of order, even as it sunk into death.

The water churned less and less as I tried to get a visual on everyone who was left. Symone was right in front of me as I made my way toward the port wall where Ella was standing on a table after having pulled Filo from the monster.

Rey was climbing up on the table, calling out to him but I couldn't hear him over the ringing in my ears from the explosion.

It all blurred together visually. I shook my head but my ears let almost nothing in, so much so that I barely was able to hear it as I saw Ella lift her gun and shoot the man she loved in the face over and over again.

15 - Infinite

We stayed on the base for the next week helping to clear the debris and pump out the infected water. We watched as Rivas reunited with Daanis. Then, in the span of a day, we had two complete funerals. I hadn't managed to coax Ella out of the ship for either one of them.

She gave us all checkups and replaced the drainers. The connection would be tighter. There would be less chance it could be pulled off in a fight. I tried to connect with her, but it was hard to get more than a few words. All she was able to think of was a cure. It's how she spent her days.

It's how she spent every night.

There was still no contact with command, either the Canadian authorities or the UN. Status satellites showed the same thing we saw before. All of us, the entire base, we were somehow 200 years in the future. We suspected the war had ended, but we had no way of knowing.

What we could see, though, was the result.

The base was led by Colonel Elkheart. She was a tallish, thin, quiet, and reserved woman in her fifties. Her hair was sleek and dark with grey roots, bundled into a long braid behind her. She was wiry and you could tell the gun at her waist wasn't for show.

She had led her people to clear this floor- the top one - on the base and done it quickly. The depressurized floor in between, filled with water and junk, had prevented her and her team from doing the same for the bottom, which is where we came in. Under ordinary circumstances, I would have spent my time talking with her one on one.

She had risen up from the ranks as a technologist before being forced into command. And, although she seemed to be an excellent delegator, she still enjoyed managing technology solutions herself.

Ladia had been gone for seven days. And Filo, too. We stood in the control center of Waaseyaagmiing and surveyed the few kilometers around us we could access visually through cameras, satellites, and other sensors as Colonel Elkheart walked us through it on her Holo.

"Basically, we're losing land mass everywhere. The lakes are deeper, including lake Simcoe. The land masses surrounding them are deteriorated. Most of the peninsulas are gone. And for all I know, this could be happening all over the world." She pointed out areas on the map that didn't match the projected visuals in front of us.

"Could this be just local?" I was trying to figure out how all this fit together. And failing.

"Sure. It could be just a few kilometers around this base. But that's unlikely. Why just here? These are all disconnected systems." Sher pointed to the screen. "That's a whole new body of water. A lake without a name."

"A tactic from the war?" Rey was doing his best to figure it out, too.

The Colonel looked over at Daanis, at the end of the table. "I don't think so. It doesn't seem like it's weaponized and I can't imagine how it would be done. There's just...more water."

Symone asked the question we were all thinking, "And those things?"

The Colonel sighed, "Everywhere. They are on land, in the water, everywhere. It's bad. And while we have no official communication. We have these." She pressed a button and a series of lines lit up on the screen.

I looked up. "What are those?"

"Requests for assistance. For help." The lines multiplied and continued. There must have been hundreds.

Rey pointed at the screen, "What do the colors mean?"

"Red are most urgent, The other colors work from there. The ones in blue are dormant."

Symone asked, "Dormant?"

Rivas spoke up, "It just means that the signal disappeared. They might still need help. Or..."

"Got it." I sighed. I stared up at the unending list scrolling across the screen. Our new world was full of water.

Water and death.

"But..."

I looked up at the Colonel and let go of my internal dialogue. There would be time to zone out later.

"We do have a few things around, though, that might interest you. C'mon."

***

The base had managed to rescue a number of other vehicles found in the water before we arrived. When he wasn't spending time with Daanis, Rivas was helping to oversee their redeployment. One of them was of real interest to us. It was an ATARAS, much like the Fearless. This one, however, seemed to be a bit of a later model. And where the Fearless had pods built around it yellow on black, this one ATARAS-31, had green.

They had cleaned it up nicely as we made our tour.

"The Triage zone is smaller. And the Lab is bigger." I noted.

"That's it, mostly, for cosmetic differences. But there are a lot under the hood." Rivas cleaned as we moved through it, pointing out to Rey and myself any areas of interest.

"The greywater reclamation is new and state-of-the-art. Every inch of the outside hull is solar generating."

We stepped back into the lounge area.

"And check this out. It wasn't working when they brought it in, but the one in the Fearless helped close the gaps. We fixed it." It was an aggregator. This one was larger, slightly more industrial looking.

But it was an aggregator.

"How is that possible?' I looked at Rey, "I mean, Filo made the one in the fearless. It was the only one."

"Maybe Manny and the rest built it from his specs?" Rey inspected it. "Or maybe it just became commonplace in the last two hundred years."

"That's insane. The technology came from the future, right?"

"Yes, just like the virus." Rey was trying to piece it together.

"What's insane is that there are two more just like this on the base." Rivas equivocated, as we stepped out. "Well, not JUST like this..."

Rey shook his head. "That's not a good sign. These are assistance vehicles. Did you add these?" He pointed to the three turrets at top, carrying massive 360 degree weaponry.

Rivas motioned for one of the techs to come over with a pad. He swiped a few times. " Nope. These do seem like recent additions but we only fixed them. We didn't add them."

"The people in these- they all fought. And it looks like they lost." Rey seemed to shrink a little.

Rivas showed me the pad, "Do you want these added to the Fearless?"

Rey glanced over at me with a tired look and nodded.

"Yes, absolutely." I handed him the pad back. I wanted to be ready, no matter what.

"Anything else you want added to this one?"

"What do you mean?" I gave Rivas a confused look.

He pat the side of the new ship. "Colonel Elkheart is giving you this ship. She's locking down the base. It'll be a pure research facility, no one in, no one out. She wants you to have the people and ships you need to make a difference."

I thought for a second. Running my hand through my hair made me realize that all I wanted was a bath and a drink and one night. Something quiet. Some time to process what my life would look like without my friends. But that wasn't going to happen.

"Good. I'll take you and Daanis."

"Got it."

"Wait. Just like that?"

He smiled. It wasn't a wide happy go lucky smile. It was the kind of smile your doctor might give you to reassure you as you began a long road to recovery. It was friendly. It wasn't happy. But it said 'we're in this together.'

"We're already packed."

***

I hugged Ella in the dining area of the Fearless. She pulled away too quickly.

My heart sunk as I tried to catch her eyes.

"You're infected."

She looked down and nodded. I pulled her closer, tightly.

"Don't. Please. I don't want to…" She pushed me away. She didn't need to tell me how it happened. It was too much to ask for her to just never get close to someone she loved.

"You have to find a cure." I took her by the shoulders.

"She will. We're going to watch out for her and make sure nothing stops it. That is our number one job, I promise." Symone dropped her bags.

I looked over at her. She looked so resolute. I believed her. "Why are you packed?"

Rey brought his bags out, too, and put them down, "We're going to take the Green Ship - the unnamed one. Rivas and Daanis are already there."

"Why? I can take that one."

"It had an aggregator. And a bigger lab. Fearless has a larger Triage Bay. And you're familiar with it. You need it."

"Rey, it's your ship." The idea of being on here alone was crushing.

"It's yours now. It's not too late, I can come with you…"

"I'll watch after Ella, no matter what." Symone lifted her rifle.

"No, I'm going to do this alone. " I looked up at the list on the monitor. The closest cluster of people.

"It's twenty people and they need help, but I think if I use the time slips I can do that. What you are doing is more important. It's the whole world. Besides, I may need to do some things that I can undo. You can't. If you set up at the staging area, I can touch base after."

"Speaking of things you can't undo, here it is." Ella handed me the baseball sized device. "It's an ototoxic gas bomb."

"Great. And you have…"

She put her hands in mine. "I don't know how long it'll last or if it's even permanent. Do you understand?"

"I do."

She handed me the black taser looking device. "This is your upgraded screecher. The controls show what's happening. All the way up is, well, everyone in range. I programmed it all in the aggregator on the ship, too."

"Amazing." I clipped them onto my belt. This was a last ditch plan, but it was a plan nonetheless. It felt better than no plan. I suddenly felt more hopeful than I had in months.

Until Rey spoke up. "If we get separated by the time dilation, this could be goodbye, you know."

I took a breath. I had been trying not to think about it. But he was right. "Have you gotten in touch with anyone?"

He shifted his bag, "No one. I can't find information. I have one satellite. I don't know the exact date. Just the year But we could start to drift the minute we separate."

"We won't. And I'll see you again. You know what to do."

"Yes, Colonel." He put his hand in mine.

I looked down. "This looks like you don't think you're going to see me again."

"It just means that I want to. It's an honor to work with you."

"You, too. You're an amazing X-O."

"Right back at you, Colonel."

I looked around the room as they got ready to leave. "That goes for all of you. It's an honor. Find an answer, please."

I grabbed Ella's hand as she made her way off the ship and pulled her toward me. I hugged her as hard as I could. There were so many things to say. I rocked back and forth as the other two left. I tried to remember when we were kids, the two of us. When I was just some lanky kid and she was already desperately trying to grow her hair out and to get people to see her as a girl. I realized I had dragged her with me my whole life because I was never ready to let her go.

And I wasn't now.

She whispered, "Remember when your mom first tried to teach us to sky dive, with parachutes?"

I dug my face into her neck and nodded.

"What's the shitty rule?" She asked.

I remembered. My mom had taught us what she called the shitty rule. Looking at these two kids who never really wanted to not do everything together. The shitty rule had to be learned.

"Someone has to go first."

Ella pulled away, finally letting go of my hand. and she walked out of the Fearless.

I followed her.

I stood outside the ship and covered them as they filed into the green ship. It did have a bigger lab, by a lot. But this felt wrong. I watched them move off. The staging area was about a half a kilometer away, far enough away to avoid the runoff of the Zeds from my first stop. Close enough to respond if needed.

I looked at the pad in my hands. The Braca Hotel. Nicknamed the infinite hotel because of its opulence. Twenty people, trapped by zombies. This had been the reddest of the transmissions. The most urgent.

I tried to calm myself, thinking about Ella working on the cure, I had to trust her. I had to put all my faith in her. I had to find my faith again. I dug back to a time when I remembered what winning felt like.

It didn't feel like this.

I took a deep breath, thinking about what I had to do next. There was something liberating about doing this part alone.

I slid into the NavPod. There was no need for stealth anymore. The job was to drag all of them out into the open. I set my location to the first stop. It wasn't far. But it did give me a chance to see the fallout from the war with my own two eyes.

It was devastation. Massive pits dotted the landscape, surrounded by residential buildings torn in two, businesses destroyed, crops burned. There was nothing alive out there, but the virus itself.

And that thrived.

Cows stood in groups, absentmindedly feeding on the ones that had been lucky enough to die right out. Their faces split open, caustic infected blood spraying from inside, brackish tendrils ushering food into their ragged maws, to be torn apart by steely robotic looking teeth.

Birds flew in animated patterns, twitching and flailing until they dropped to the ground and limped toward snakelike pools of bloody water, ripping pieces of meat from their banks, searching for anything alive enough to give them sustenance.

The sounds of animal echolocation swam through the air, warbling, oscillating tones meant to bounce off surfaces and return to whatever creator stood, waiting to assess their surroundings and eat, pounce, destroy. It created an alien-like atmosphere, giving the illusion that you were driving across some far distant planet looking for a human-staged base, trying to find something, anything familiar.

I moved up to the front of the hotel. This would be MY first staging area.

The hotel was huge, the first few floors obscured with junk, dirt, and debris, dark and foreboding, while a tower, hundreds of meters tall, rose up, surrounded by glass, lit from the inside, glistened in the sunlight. If you looked closely, you could see the outlines of dark shapes rushing through the tower. There was no way to know, though, if they were human or infected.

I centered the ship in front of the hotel about one hundred meters away and hit the gas. The Fearless jerked forward faster than I had driven her in the past. Within seconds, the panel read over Two hundred fifty KPH as I slammed into the front of the building. An abrupt stop sent me ripping from my seat belt, flying forward smashing my head into the front monitor. Blood ran down into my eyes as my neck cracked. I twisted it as far as I could to see the thick column in front of me. My vision began to fade to black while I recorded the rest. A wide open, mostly glass covered area about twenty meters to my right. The black closed in like a blanket falling over me and I died.

***

I snapped back to right before the start of my drive into the building. I was starting to get good at observing the situation right before I died so I could make sense of it all. This was going to be the only way I could use the advantage of my time slips. I looked down at the lower monitor on the dashboard and parsed the information there. A few things started to make sense but not in the front of my mind yet.

It was all nagging at me, making me wish I had time to parse it.

I drove over about 20 meters to the right and pointed myself at the hotel again, hitting the gas. I flinched as the ship slammed into the area in front of me, experiencing remarkably little resistance from the wall, and surging toward the center of a spacious foyer. I pulled back on the brakes and the Fearless began slowing, the back pulling out to starboard and nearly spinning out in the center of the room.

I could see about seven of the Zeds moving in from the shadows. A massive skylight above and an ascending tower of windows made the room bright - too bright for them. I spun the newly added turrets around and lit up the room some more. The beasts ran toward me and died in a shower of bullets and coherent light while the turrets swept the room. I advanced a few meters until I saw it.

A pit opened up in front of me, about twice the diameter of the Fearless. Bloody water shot up from it with each Zed who was shot and fell into it. I put the brakes down and spun the turrets around, firing only in that direction. I felt a jerk and looked down at the monitors. The back cameras were showing three of the creatures pushing the Fearless forward. Despite the brakes, I felt myself losing ground, heading toward the open pit. Creatures in front were pulling as well, determined to drop the ship into the hole in the floor of the hotel foyer.

I backed up with all the power in the ship, but it was too late. The front dipped to the left as it spun, moving toward the gorge, spinning and tipping into it.

From the side monitor the last thing I saw was a man, standing in between the creatures, directing them, as the fearless descended into the water-filled hole in front of it and every monitor went black.

15 - Merged

I woke up on dry land in a large shimmery blue room with no clothes on.

All around me I could see the glow of liquid, refracting the dim light, bathing everything in a somber blue movement that felt alive and strangely soothing. I had no idea how I'd gotten there.

Did i die?

I don't remember dying. And I didn't remember this room. For the first time in a long time, nothing here was familiar. I reached down to my belt before realizing I had no belt. The room was hot and womblike. I cleared my throat. An inviting voice seemed to fade in.

"Colonel Pinga. You are awake." The voice echoed through the room. I couldn't find the source. It was somber and peaceful but alien. With an accent I couldn't place.

"You know who I am?"

"We do. Very much so."

"Can I have my clothes?"

"Yes, of course."

A tendril of water snaked down from the ceiling and formed into a perfect column. It opened in the front, revealing my clothes, folded and looking none the worse for wear. I reached in delicately and grabbed them, putting my pants on. They were dry.

"I had tools with me. Things I needed." Suddenly I realized I had been wearing a drainer. I reached behind me.

It was gone.

"Really important tools."

"Ah. your weapons. You won't need them here."

A wave of questions racked my brain. Somehow one of them won out barely over the others. "How did I get here?"

"This is the end. In a way. All roads lead here."

"I don't remember getting here."

"Well, you did die a number of times on approach. We thought we would spare you the memories of those details. I saw images flashing across the water. It showed me dying time after time throughout the hotel, trying to reach the people I was looking for. I felt angry for a moment. Those memories were all I really had. They were my only advantage in figuring out what to do.

And they were stolen from me.

"Who are you?"

I am called Merged. I am well known where I come from. I forget that this is not that."

I started moving toward the voice. "Can I see you?"

"You can. If you want. I know you will ask where I come from."

"You're very smart. That was about to be my very next question."

"Well. First things first."

The wall of water in front of me faded to dark blue. There were sparks, seemingly, within it, like small arcs of electricity. They grew closer, as though spinning toward the edge of the water.

I could see now, the entire room was enclosed with this animated waterfall. The surface tension kept the water at bay, almost as though gravity had been perverted to curve a lake around the entire room.

The water cleared and I saw a creature walking toward me, from beyond it. At first, I jerked backward.

He was infected.

But as I looked closer it became clear that this person in front of me, despite having all the physical characteristics of an infected, was rational. His face was featureless. No mouth or nose, no eyes or even occipital ridges. When he spoke, nothing moved. But as he stood there, atop spindly legs, his long slick arms folded, his face split open down the center, revealing a familiar sight- a reddish maw, cavernous and encircled with metallic teeth.

He seemed to breathe. He was breathing the water swirling around him.

"There's no reason to be scared."

"Where are you from?"

"If I wanted to be poetic, I would say now. My people are evolving in the very oceans around you. We are becoming our perfect selves."

"In 800 years? Nothing evolves like that in 800 years."

"Ha. 800 years in your future. That is where we are now. We are at the hub."

"Wait, this is 800 years in the future? How long have I been here, fighting, dying?" My heart sunk to my knees. Everything I knew would be gone. All of it. And I remembered nothing."

"I don't think you really understand how any of this works. Each of your missions is in its own proprietary timeline."

"To lead me here?"

"Yes, actually." The wall of water was alive with situations, some including me, maddeningly unfamiliar. it was a biography of me told through events I didn't remember. And I couldn't use any of that information.

"So where are YOU from?" I tried to read the creature's face.

I couldn't.

"One day, 800 million years in your Earth's future, it will be a paradise. A planet covered in warm water, filled with food that requires nearly no labor. And endless amount of space for my people…"

"Evolved from fish…"

"Well, yes. We remember a time before you humans made yourselves untenable. This hub was built to give you a choice. A place, far in our distant past, where we could connect with you, those we used to share this world with.

"And do what?"

"Give you a chance. To follow us into the future. Or to die right here."

"How do we do that?"

"This is the pentaculum." as he spoke, a device rose up from the floor. It looked to be a five sided table with a kind of crystal in the center. Under the surface of the table, behind a shimmering glassine water, were items, things I could barely make out.

"What is this?"

"The pentaculum is your choice. Inside it are five of our greatest discoveries. Five gifts."

I moved closer. Two of the slots in the table had been broken open. Used.

"I don't understand. Pentaculum?"

"It was named by the American. I assumed you'd know."

I looked up. "Wait, American? What American? I spun around and felt something slam into the back of my head. The light in the room sucked into itself leaving a pinprick as I felt my knees hit the floor.

***

I woke up on the floor a few meters away from the Pentaculum. The room felt warmer, even more like an organic place.

There was a man hulking over the device. He looked like he might have been trying to break into it. He was in a one piece blue military outfit, something a pilot might wear. But he didn't strike me as a pilot. I remembered what the creature had said about the American as I saw the eagle patch on his arm.

I tried unsuccessfully to extricate myself. Something felt different. The room felt different. I suddenly wondered if I had lost any more time.

"Hey, dumbshit."

He responded without pulling away from what he was doing, "Hey, aboot. I was wondering when you were going to wake up. You want to stop this little ride?"

I thought for a second. I didn't need to let him know how little I remembered. "Nope."

"Ok. He turned to me and pulled a knife out of his belt. His hands were wrapped up in makeshift bandages. He stepped over to me and knelt down grabbing my face with one hand, stabbing the knife directly into my right eye with the other. He moved the knife back and forth while I screamed, as though he were coring an apple. Blood streamed across my face and blinded my other eye. I heard my own screams for what seemed like an interminable amount of time and then everything went quiet. The last thing I felt was the ridge of the knife scraping my ocular orbit.

***

I shook myself awake. I looked up. He was back to his efforts to break into the futuristic device.

"Did you like that? I bet that hurt. I'm getting really good at killing you. You know." He looked over at me with an evil grin, "making it count."

"Did I do the hands?" I asked, looking at his bandaged hands.

"No. Try to keep up."

I had to agree with him that I had a disturbingly small amount of information. And no real way to get more except through this idiot. Honestly, I had no knowledge that he was an idiot. I just hoped, with all the fervent wistfulness of someone who would like nothing more than for their enemy to be sort of stupid.

"Trying to get the other three?"

"Just one more, really." He turned to me. In fact, you can help. Why don't you... you know" He made a motion with the knife.

I looked at him confused, "kill myself?"

"No, dumbass. Jesus. Cut your thumb off."

"Why would I do that?"

"Not all of you returns from the dead, I guess. Look, the Pentaculum... " He dragged me up by the ropes. "Is this thing here. And you choose your gift - up top. Then you pay for it." He dropped me back down. It seemed like this guy had possibly been here a little too long. He did seem starved for human interaction. I could use that.

"So, what is the payment?" I looked up at him with an expression I hope translated to friendly in his current state of mind.

"This." He put his left hand in his mouth and bit down on the bandage. With his right he tried to unwrap it. Suddenly, it became clear why. His hand was covered in brown, caked on dried blood, spreading across every finger and down his wrist, emanating from the space where his thumb once was. "Freely given. A thumb. Fucked up, Right?"

"Shit. You cut off your own thumb?"

His eyes bulged widely. He raised his other hand, wrapped just like the first."

"Ah. Both your thumbs. Got it."

He tried to wrap his hand back up. I made a motion to stand up. I tried to look at him reassuringly as I hopped over to the device. "You got the first two. Where are they? And what are they?"

"You don't remember any of this, huh? I guess dying really hurts."

"Oh, it's awful." I winked at him. I suspected that this was not 100% working. "Where did the guy from the future go?" I motioned to the wall of water. I admit I was looking all around for my cache of weapons. Nothing.

"Oh. That's really an interactive type hologram. He'll run through the whole thing again tomorrow." He waved over the device. "But…"

A smaller version of the merged appeared as a hologram over the device. "In the first slot, two vials, one containing the larger cells, one the smaller ones, combine them for a tool that will wreak havoc with your enemies, tearing them down, destroying them and forcing them to fear you."

I looked down and saw the slot darkened. Above it, in a ridge, was a severed thumb, sunk into the poly glass of the surface.

"It gave you the virus. Like some kind of vending machine?"

"No. It sent it back in time. 800 years. Or it's doing it. I don't understand how it all works."

"This virus, all of it. It's you?"

"It worked. A weapon of war. A way to bring my enemies down." He held his hand. "It worked."

He waved his hand over the next next slot. The hologram faded and reappeared over that slot. "Coherent light weapons that will make short work of any war, bring your enemies to their knees."

"And win." he looked at me. He seemed so proud, like a little child that had finished his milk. He believed he deserved to feel pride. I moved my elbow over above the third slot and waved. The smaller version of the creature appeared again. "In slot three, the cure to the viruses, what is needed to save those you love and wipe it away."

"The cure. Are you telling me this thing will send the cure back in time if we select this?"

He nodded. "The cure."

I realized that the other two were there untouched. "Cut my hands free."

"Not gonna happen."

"You want my thumb, don't you. You want one more of these." I realized that's what he was motioning about. Not killing myself.

Removing my thumb.

He reached over and cut one cord, freeing my left hand. I waved it over the fourth item and the tiny golem appeared. He seemed to be getting more philosophical, more heady as it went on. "Choose the fourth one and you will have the keys to a true and lasting inevitable peace. One that endures for generations and beyond."

I closed my eyes. I could feel the water welling up behind my eyelids. My brain raced. I was so confused. I leaned in against the pentaculum, feeling sick. I whispered.

"You could have had that. You could have sent that back. And you didn't." I looked at him. "Instead, you sent monsters."

"You judge me because you're losing. What would have happened if we had lost?"

I felt something coiling up inside me. I didn't understand anything. It didn't make sense. I lifted my free hand over the fifth slot.

The water wall around us filled with images of people, dressed in rags, dirty. I could tell immediately. These were the people trapped here. I counted 20 of them. The creature's voice rang out as I stared into their faces. "Twenty American Citizens, starving, in various stages of health, some with not long to live, hoping for release. One way or the other."

The American looked at me and laughed. Thumblessly, he pointed at me. "Peace. You see. This is why we'll never have it. There's always something you want more, isn't there? Always something a little bit shinier."

My head was swimming. I looked up and down the row of faces. The imagery lit the room. And that's when I saw it. On a stool a few meters behind me. My tools. The things I needed.

I stared at him. "Why do you need my thumb? You have the two things you wanted.

"I almost do." He turned his head and showed me the drainer. It was mine. He had taken it off of me when I was unconscious."What good is winning if you're not alive to see it. Don't worry. I'll make sure all the right people have the cure. And the wrong ones?" He shrugged.

I opened my hand. He handed me the knife and moved around the device.

I could see the area I was meant to deposit my thumb in. Over the last few months, I'd gotten pretty used to pain, even considering it a passage, a journey that was uniquely mine. I looked at him. I lifted the blade with my free hand and brought it down on the area right in front of the knuckle of my right thumb. Red washed across my eyes as the pain screamed out. I dug it into my skin, deeper and deeper, carving out a ridge on my hand. I felt the bone bend and snap and I lifted it to my mouth and bit down hard, severing it finally.

I dropped it from my mouth to the table staring into his eyes. He grinned and began to make his way over to slide the detached appendage into the groove in front of me. I spit in his face and dragged it across the top of the table to the final slot, inserting it.

The voice boomed out as the wall dimmed. "Congratulations. You have chosen to send the people back. They will arrive back in the past unharmed."

I dove toward my weapons, leaving a trail of blood across the undulating floor. I lifted the bomb up with my free hand and threw it. With my debilitated hand I palmed the small black taser shaped device.

The bomb hit the floor, just beyond the Pentaculum and a wave of smoke poured from it. I looked up to see the American screaming at me, and for a moment, could hear him clear as day.

Then, my brain caught fire. My ears felt like they were swallowing themselves up. I inhaled the gas and felt it do its work, ripping through my brain, destroying every piece of my brain's hardware to hear anything. I spit blood on the floor, looking up to see the American laughing. He pointed to the drainer. The gas left him unaffected as it tore through my head and rendered me completely deaf.

I imagined a pilot tone. Thin and wispy, sharp, as every sound died out. I lifted the black device and turned it on, watching his face explode in pain. His hands cupped his ears, as blood poured out from under them. HIs eyes bulged outward, the wells behind them filling with blood and pus. He fell on the ground and rolled around, trying to crawl toward me, unable to. The deathly silence filled my head, creating a wide open, airy space filled by nothing, a vacuum, empty, imperceptible. I searched my brain for the meaning of sound but there was nothing.

I crawled to the Pentaculum and lifted myself up. The American was twitching on the floor. I could see on the device that it was still screeching, still sending out its destructive noise. I dropped it on the top of the table.

Reaching for the knife, I held it in my other hand, tied still to itself.

I lifted it it straight up in the air and drove it, blade downward, into the hinge connecting my free thumb to its mooring. I stabbed again and again, feeling the bones crack under the blade and then, finally, lifted it to my mouth again to bite free.

I spit it on the table and moved it to the slot for number three. I pressed it down as hard as I could and the Pentaculum lit up. A voice seemed to transmit itself to my brain. "Congratulations. You have chosen the cure. The cure will be sent back in lieu of the virus if you have chosen both. It will arrive in your native time period."

I realized now, that I was fully deaf, that I had never heard sounds in this room. It was all being transmitted directly to my brain. I pulled at my shirt, ripping strips off to wrap around my hands. I leaned down on top of the device.

One slot was still lit. I stared into it. It seemed impossibly beautiful. I reached out as I began to cry, leaving behind the only thing in the Pentaculum that I really ever wanted. The only one of the five I'd ever dreamed about.

My head slammed into it as I fell to the ground.

17 - Home

I woke up in the back middle bunk of the fearless in the dark. It took a second for my eyes to adjust to the near absolute black and see the room around me.

I was alone.

I looked down at my arms. No blood. My hands were all there. Thumbs and all. I grunted.

I did it again.

I could hear again. I felt all over. Nothing was broken. Nothing was missing.

Nothing.

I wanted a shower. But more than anything, I wanted to know where everyone was. I needed to know where I was. I stepped into the central corridor and shielded my eyes from the light. The ship was powered down and I didn't see or hear anyone.

"Guys?"

Nothing. I walked through the Triage Zone and out the starboard bay. And there it was.

Sounds of life.

The Fearless was parked on a street in what looked to be a residential area. The house to my right had three blue cars out front and 2 younger teenagers playing in the yard. They didn't seem to have noticed me or the massive tank-like structure yet.

I walked around the front to see a tiny strip mall across the street. My stomach grumbled. Right in front of me was Hog's Back restaurant, serving Canadian and Italian food.

I was in Ottawa. I was home. Not only that, I was back in the past.

I was back where I started. I thought for a moment. Could I have expired from my original choice to leave? That made no sense. I usually snapped back to proximal decision points. It didn't seem like I had died on the Pentaculum.

I moved forward, almost mechanically. The restaurant was fascinating. But if I really wanted information, the business to the right of it was the place to go.

A buzzer rang out as I opened the door. The main room was longer than it seemed outside and it was about a third full of people. It felt weirdly familiar, but that was a feeling I was beginning to get used to.

Why was nearly everything familiar to me?

I looked around for the counter to the right in the center of the store. In front of it was a large seating area where a few kids played video games. The guy at the counter was skinny and tall with short dreadlocks and a name tag that said "Zio" He was completely enthralled in a book he held open in his lap. He wore a rumpled grey T-shirt that had all the earmarks of being his favorite shirt. On the front was a scene from YuGiOh.

The card game, not the anime.

Without looking up from his book, he greeted me. "Welcome to Gamezetera 2, How can I help you?"

Suddenly a girl screamed. I turned to see her barreling through the door. "You fuckers have to see this. Fucking Now."

I piled out with Zio and the rest and we all stood looking at the Fearless. I could honestly see where all the excitement was coming from. On this tiny street it was a massive physical object. Zio shook his head.

"What the fuck is that?"

I looked over at the smaller girl who had screamed earlier. Her Name Tag said "La Raza." I was guessing that it wasn't her real name.

Given where we were, it was likely it was her gamer tag. She walked over to him while about thirty people stared at the Fearless, talking together. Her voice was shrill and cutting and I didn't expect what she said next.

"Zio, dude. It's the motherfucking Fearless. "

Suddenly, my head felt light. I pushed my way through the people, grabbing La Raza's arm. My hand was like a claw, clamping down harder than I had intended.

"How do you know the name of that vehicle?"

She stared at me, first in anger and then in something that looked like realization.

"Holy shit, everyone. This is her. Everybody. This is Tomi Pinga. This is Fearless-17."

I felt my legs start to buckle as the group of people swarmed all around me. I fell into a tunnel of black. Looking up I saw faces as the black closed in. The last thing I saw was La Raza's face.

"Holy fucking shit."

And the dark took over.

**

The girl I knew as La Raza was shoving miniature ice cubes into my mouth. I tried to sit up but my head hit the bottom of the table. I was in a booth, sealed with red leather. Wasn't sure right away if this wasn't another time jump. But I had just passed out.

I didn't die.

"Dude. When was the last time you ate?" Zio offered me a bowl of soup and I took it.

"Where are we?"

La Raza sat back down across from me. "We share a back room with Asia Garden. It comes in handy. Eat something. I got this. I'm a huge fan."

I sat up completely. It was egg drop soup. Kind of my favorite, honestly. I didn't remember the last time I ate. "You're a fan of me?"

Zio answered, "She's not. She thinks you're the person you're cosplaying as. She has reality issues."

Apparently, so did I, "So I'm cosplaying as who?"

Zio looked back down. I could see he'd brought his book. "As whom."

"Shut up." La Raza threw a fortune cookie at him. "You. You're Tomi Pinga. You're like the greatest player in history. You beat Amzed."

I beat what? "I had a potsticker. I was starting to feel alive again. Even as I was being told I was a character. She pulled a disk out of her bag. It was dark and had an apocalyptic image on the front with something I could dimly make out as a vehicle.

The Fearless.

"American Zombies. It's one of my favorite horror-based games. You were the first to beat this, only a few days ago. The infinite hotel. The Merged."

"Wait, what?" I was honestly confused. I thought back to the massive structure with all those rooms. The Braca. An Infinite hotel? I didn't remember most of it. But I remembered the room at the end.

"Yes. The Hotel Braca. It's the Infinite Hotel. They haven't built an expansion pack yet with new levels. That was the last level. You fucking beat the game. The deaf gambit. Wild."

"How did I beat it?"

"The objectives?" She pointed to the writing on the back. It read "Your objective is to save as many people as possible."

Had I really done that?

"You won."

"And you've been watching?"

"The stream? Yeah. It's monetized so I even donated a few times. Money talks."

"You're both fucking delusional." Zio didn't bother to look up.

I squinted across the table, "Why?"

Zio sighed and put his book down on the table. He clearly meant business. He addressed La Raza authoritatively as he shook a finger at me, "Because she's not Tomi Pinga. I saw an article on Tomi Pinga last month and, I'm sorry, that ain't her."

"Wait, you saw an article?" None of this was making any sense. I'm in a video game, but I'm not running the video game?.

"What article?" La Raza leaned in.

Zio stood up. "C'mon."

***

I stood by the Fearless. Only one or two people still gathered around, some taking pictures with their phones. Zio and La Raza met me on the street.

"Can I leave this here?"

Zio hrumphed, "Sure. and I wouldn't pay those, either." He pointed at the two tickets that had already been taped to the left side window. "Nobody can tow this thing. It'll be fine. C'mon."

He threw his keys up in the air and just missed catching them. He did that again twice before we got to his car, an old red Honda Civic.

La Raza looked at me apologetically, "I can't sit in the back. I get carsick." I sighed and slid into the back seat. It was only twenty minutes away. And the conversation on the way was enlightening. We talked about the game a little. And finally, about me.

"So I'm a character from a video game, but I'm playing the game?" I was honestly confused.

Zio shook his head, "nope."

"Yes, in a way." La Raza was on her knees turned backward. The game has a character generator. You are the game's version of Tomi Pinga. Or that's what you're dressed as."

"I'm really just dressed as me."

"Well, that's what the outfit is. The hair, the face, all of it. Is that a wig?" she reached out to grab my hair. I put my hands up.

"It is not. This is my hair. It's my real hair."

La Raza shrugged apologetically. "It's brilliant. I mean, you look just like how Tomi Pinga is supposed to look."

"People just watch other people playing the game?"

"Not the shitty ones," Zio was putting almost all his attention into driving.

"No, not them. But the greats, yeah. And Fearless-17 is one of the greatest. We didn't know her real name- your name- until a few levels ago."

"And it says, in the game, that my name is Tomi Pinga?"

"Yes, Canadian Military. Colonel Pinga. There is a whole backstory. The crash. The death of Commander Herman."

"It says that? That he died?"

"Yes, he died. In the game, you and the others survived. And you got a new command. The others came with you. That's your backstory."

"Ok, where are they now?"

La Raza looked at Zio. He was clearly frustrated. And unwilling to help. "We don't know. You went offline once you won. You beat the game. You cleared the hotel. The people. You even got the cure. The stream is over."

"But isn't it an open universe game?" I was exhausting everything I knew about gaming.

La Raza looked excited, "It is. You're right. I mean you could still do side quests or anything, really. You just...haven't."

"What about the remaining team members?"

La Raza looked at me. "NPCs. You made them."

"NPCs," I felt a little sick to my stomach.

Zio sighed. He pointed to a sign hanging over the passenger side dash. It said "NPC" along with the definition and an arrow, directed at the passenger. "Non. Playable. Characters. NPCs."

"And I'm offline?"

"Yes."

"And ok. We're here." Zio pulled up and turned the car off. "The home of Tomi Pinga. Or not. But this is where the article says it should be."

I looked at the red A frame while La Raza fidgeted uneasily, "Your house."

***

We stood in front of the unassuming single family home. It was small, probably only seven hundred square feet. At first glance, most of the forward face of the building was a shocking red. As I stood there, though, it seemed to become more comfortable, more homey. It wasn't the red of sports cars or sleek little toy fire trucks. It wasn't even the red of cheap Chinese restaurant booth leather. It wasn't the kind of red that said speed and bluster and power. It was the red from tiny kids pictures of barns and houses drawn with red crayon on lined paper, pasted to the fridge.

"I can't say I understand what's going on here, but do you want me to come with?"

I looked at the smaller girl next to me. "What does 'La Raza' mean, anyway?"

"Oh. it sort of means 'the people.' It's all of us. For me, it's my tribe, my people. It's gamers."

"Funny." She looked so young. But she was a force. "I'm Inuit. Part, anyway. In Inuk, the word 'Inuit' means 'the people.' So, when you talk, everyone is inuit. It's like you are pulling everyone in."

"The people."

I looked up. "But I like it. It fits you. The tag." I took a deep breath and began exploring my memories around the house. Like most things this last few months of my life, it DID seem familiar.

But I'd learned not to trust that instinct. It wasn't doing anything for me. It wasn't making any of this easier.

I felt like someone whose feet were being pulled out from under them. I remembered being underwater, under the Huron, the room filling up and the current pulling at my feet.

I shook my head and made my way up the walkway to the front door. I turned the knob easily and pushed open the door. The air felt warm and humid. The room in front of me was dark and seemingly unlived in. It was fastidiously clean. A steady beeping beckoned me to the next room. Through the arch in front of me, I passed a spotless if sparse kitchen.

The beeping was louder now, more clearly coming from the far doorway.

Off the kitchen was a den.

I hope it makes sense If I'm overly clinical in talking about what i found in that Den, because there are things I can explain well and things I just can't. In the Den was a bed, nearly empty except for a pillow in the center.

"You look more like her. More than the last one."

I spun around and she was standing right there.

My Mom.

My heart started beating faster.

"What...?"

"More like my Tomi." She put her purse down on a chair by the door. She took off her shawl. "Did you get what you came for?"

"Mom?"

"Yes, I'm the great Tomi Pinga's mother." She stepped into the kitchen. I could still see her through a cutaway in the wall. "Do you want some tea or are you one of the dangerous ones? You know. The unhinged ones." She waved her hands while she said that. She looked exactly as I remembered. Just a little older. She looked to be in her late sixties.

Her hair was still dark and smooth, 'those inuit genes' she would say. Her eyes were black and piercing, set widely, powerful. I remembered growing up, thinking that this was the strongest woman in the world. She seemed tired now, if anything, but bristling with that power. It was so clearly her. I wanted to run to her and wrap my arms around her.

"Thank you, ma'am."

"Oh, ma'am, is it? You're a polite one."

"I was raised well."

"Not well enough to not go barging into people's homes."

"I'm sorry, ma'am."

She handed me a cup of tea. It was royal tea- smooth and white. Before I tasted it, I knew it would be sweet and creamy. I took the cup. I felt like my hands should be shaking, but they weren't. "What happened?"

"Well. You probably know most of it." She walked over to the bed. I'd been trying not to think about what was in the bed. At first glance it seemed to be a pillow, a tiny one, wrapped in white gauze. As I looked down, I saw a person.

It was Tomi Pinga. Her face was nearly unrecognizable under the gauze. She had one arm, descending into a fingerless hand. Her other arm and both legs were stumps, missing. She was burned and red under the dressing. She seemed unable to move. She stared upward, immobile. One eye was visible. Open. Seemingly unseeing.

"The crash?"

"Yes, it's funny. My Tomi was always a brilliant pilot. She flew since she was practically a baby. It took a bomb shaped like a whole damn plane to hurt her." She fluffed the pillow and began to look through her dressings for anything she could do.

Anything she could fix to make her daughter feel better.

I turned my eyes away. In the corner, I saw the game console. And the disk that La Raza had shown me. American Zombies.

"That damned game." My mother shook her head. "She's been hooked up to it for the last few years. I helped her make her character. That's why it looks so much like her. You do- you look like the character." She shook her finger at me. "But you aren't my daughter."

My heart sunk involuntarily hearing her say that. If I wasn't her daughter, what was I? Was anything in my life true? What was even happening here?

"She's gotten pretty famous in the past few months. You're the third one that's showed up, wanting to take a look at the original. "

I took a sip of my tea. It was good. "The game. It looks like it's running so quickly."

"Yeah. Her cousin sort of supercharged it. It's the thing that makes her happy. It's what she likes. Her cousin added some code to it. Gave her a hundred lives."

I felt a weight in my chest. "A hundred lives. I didn't know you could do that."

"Well, nowadays, you can do a lot. But she plays with her mind. She runs it with her head. I don't understand how it works, but I'm grateful."

"You are? For the game?"

"It means she's really still in there. She's alive. She's someone still. Oh, I know she's my daughter. I can feel it. But she's winning, like my Tomi always did."

"Winning the game?"

"Oh, she's going to. You can tell your cosplay gamer friends that. My daughter. She wins. That's what she does." She looked at me and then down to the figure in the bed. "Don't let all this fool you. I like to think of her with a hundred lives. The things she could do."

I finished my tea and tried to turn my brain off for a second. Nothing here made sense.

"Did you finish your tea?" She looked at me and I remembered my mom, younger, laughing, flying next to me, the stick in her hand, like some kind of athlete to me, in my mind. She was a hundred feet tall. She was the goddess of the sky. She was a Pinga before I was. She was everything before I was. I felt the weight in her eyes today, caring for the tiny desiccated body of the daughter she loved. I wanted to tell her what a hero she was. I wanted to say something. I looked at her.

"Yes, ma'am."

"Can you get the hell out of my house now?"

I took a deep breath and my feet began to move, as if on their own.

"Yes, ma'am."

She walked me to the door. I stood at the door, in the light, waiting for her to close it behind me.

"Does she need anything? Do you need anything?"

Then I saw it. Something on her face that recognized something in me as part of her daughter. Something that saw beyond my face and my bumbling efforts to connect and found the real me. And it happened because she wanted it. I realized that talking to me, someone who looked so elusively like the daughter she loved so much, was a guilty pleasure for her. She seemed to lean in and yearn for it, even as she knew it was a scam, a willing misdirection. She wanted to say something, anything, to draw it out, and so did I. That wasn't a cup of tea, it was a beacon, a torch in the dark, hoping for someone to catch her, to pick her back up again. I wanted to give her something, but I couldn't think of anything.

"We'll be ok. You take care of yourself."

I started to walk away,

"Just remember."

I stopped and looked back at her. I could tell how much every word hurt.

"The person you're all... dressed up as. This person you look like today. She's not some mindless vacant celebrity dancing in front of people for applause. She's good. She's someone who spent her life helping people. If you want to do right by that outfit, you do that. You go help people. You gotta earn those clothes."

I saw through the blur in my eyes, her hand slowly closing the door. "I will," I whispered. I stood there for a few minutes but the door stayed shut. The house seemed bigger now. It felt more familiar.

It felt real.

I moved down the walkway where Zio and La Raza stood, leaning up against the car, the taller one still immersed in his book. I leaned against the car hood, right next to La Raza. She was so awake and alive.

"So, how did that go?"

"It's a little complicated." After a second, I turned to her and asked.

"Can you show me this game?"

100 WAYS THE WORLD ENDS

18- AmZed

The game, American Zombies, was developed by a Canadian game developer named Xenox at the height of the war. Fans called it AmZed or AMZero for short. Much of the history in it leading up to the war was accurate. But in the world of the game, the world I had experienced, The United States had made a compact with a species of creature from 800 million years in the future called the Livre whose goal for the planet, to turn it into their watery home, aligned well enough with theirs.

This explained the absolute dominance the Americans had enjoyed in the game as well as the bizarre situations I found myself in, again and again, as we tried to bring resources and safety to people.

In reality, there were no creatures. There was no Livre - no virus. And even with the help of troops from Russia and North Korea, the US had lost the war, pulling back over a year ago. Canada had reverted back to a relatively peaceful place, but many of the areas along the border, for both countries, were full of people starving, hurting, trying to rebuild where resources were less available than they would like.

None of that answered the questions in front of me. And as I sat in the back lounge of the Fearless, listening to La Raza talk, installing the game onto the ship's computer, I realized that I didn't even know who I was. And if I thought about it too much, my head hurt.

"This is the coolest thing I've ever seen."

She was bouncing up and down on the back couch, I considered telling her not to, but why shouldn't she have fun?

"It's pretty neat."

"Zio's making big bucks charging folks to get their picture with it in the parking lot now. You could clean up if you let them inside."

"Let's hold off on that for now." I thought for a second. "Hey, how many lives do you usually have in a game like that?"

"Lives? That depends. You can earn more. But something like three is standard. Or more if there are multiple levels."

I sat down next to her. She continued jumping. "I had a hundred lives. I thought I was going back in time."

"Well, in a way, you were."

"A hundred different chances to do better. And I still couldn't save everybody."

"No offense," She sat down next to me. The couch felt oddly still without the bouncing,"But none of us get to save everyone. It's just a hundred different endings, really."

I looked at her. She seemed impossibly young. "So, Hey, bouncy. What's your real name?"

"Promise not to fucking make fun?"

"I do not really promise anything." I watched her face light up whenever I played. There was a kind of kindness to her that shone through her fidgety demeanor and sailor's mouth. She couldn't have been more than twenty.

"Ok, I promise. No laughing at you."

"It's Jesenia. The boys used to call me 'yes.' Wishful thinking. You know. Like 'yes, baby.'"

"I get it. I think that's pretty."

"Yuk. I don't need pretty." Her phone buzzed and she slid down off the couch. "Ooh. everyone is here."

I looked up. This didn't seem like the right time for a brainstorm, but it looked like I was going to get one anyway.

***

We stepped into the Gamezetera front door and Zio locked it behind us.

"Can you guys afford to be closed right now?"

He laughed, "We'll be fine. We have pretty much no overhead. We'll make it up."

"So, who do we got?" I looked around the room. There were five other people who showed up.

La Raza pointed to an older woman, about forty. She had long dark dreadlocks and an open, wise face. "Everyone except her works here on and off. This is Dr. Florida Kinley. She's a researcher at UOttowa. In the science department. And my teacher"

"Professor," I reached my hand out. "Thank you for taking the time." I looked around the room. "Thank all of you.

A young inuit girl with short, punky black hair looked over at La Raza, "Is this really her? This is Fearless-17?"

Florida answered authoritatively, "We think she is. And it's more than that."

We made our way to the conversation pit in front of the checkout. "What do you think I am?"

"Well, she started, sliding into a chair, "are you familiar with the concepts of simulated realities?"

I looked around the room. I was the only one not nodding. "I think I'm in the minority here when I say I'm not." I found myself wishing that Ella were here. Or Filo. And suddenly a wave of sadness washed over me. For a second, I couldn't breathe.

The inuit girl was excited, "The conversation's been going on for a while about simulated realities. And if we live in one. People have gone back and forth on it."

Zio piped up from the counter, "Tell her what that is."

La Raza was to my right. She leaned in. "ok, so when a civilization becomes advanced enough, they will find the need to develop simulations of reality, little miniature worlds. For testing hypotheses or running probabilities…"

"Or entertainment." a boy of about seventeen sat across from me in a Pokemon shirt. He wore a nametag that said "Xylocaine," suggesting he was working today, too.

"Right," La Raza continued, "so these open universe games, they are like universe simulations- some more low res, some really real and accurate. Like Amzed, that has real world physics and everything."

"AmZed. The game I come from. So, what's the difference between a video game and a simulation?"

Dr. Kinly fielded that one, "Well, in a way, nothing. A video game, if sufficiently advanced, can act as a universe simulator. It can maybe even fool a sentience that is living in it, convincing it that this universe is real."

"Real like everyone here right now?" I looked up.

"Well, that's just it." Xykocaine picked up. "Are we real?"

La Raza's voice rang out, "for a simulation to be effective, the thinkers in it have to believe it's real."

"I thought the game was real. But this…" I waved my hands, "IS real, isn't it?"

This was sort of Dr. Kinley's area of expertise. "There is a scientist named Nick Bostron who was presented with this problem. His conclusion is interesting and I think, valid,"

"Ok." I was willing to listen to anything.

"There are, potentially, an infinite number of 'Real' Universes.' out there."

"Natural universes that are not artificially simulated." Zio jumped in.

"Right. Dr. Boston is a mathematician. He speculated that there was nothing preventing any universe with intelligent thinkers in it from developing an artificial simulated reality."

"Probably more than one." The girl pointed out. A Velma looking girl to her right perked up.

"And there could be many many sentient peoples in any real universe. As well, nothing is stopping people in a simulated universe from creating their OWN simulations."

"So," The doctor concluded, "while the number of 'real' realities is potentially infinite, the number of simulated ones is potentially many times infinity."

"And," Zio intoned, putting his book down. "So the odds of any one of us being in a simulated reality are far higher than those of us being in a naturally occurring one."

"Assuming we really have any idea what 'naturally occurring' even means." Velma finished.

I paused for a minute and stared out at them, in a circle. "Shit. So, you think that your OWN universe here is simulated, too?" The rules are so different. I think.

The Doctor pursed her lips.

I hadn't really explained well. I tried again. "In the...Game world, I kept dying and returning. If I made a decision that led to my death, time would reverse and I would have the chance to make that decision again."

"100 lives. That was the program. And she had multiple lives because she kept her health up in the game. Plus a little hack." La Raza shot back.

"My health?"

Velma tried to find an example on her phone. "It's like three numbers. From 0 to 999. You can see it everywhere."

"And the missions, too, kept jumping forward in time." A part of me felt like I was losing my mind. How could everyone be sitting here, acting like this was all normal. I thought back to the times I'd seen that number.

"They do that," Zio offered, "You move forward in time until you meet the final boss."

"The merged." La Raza whispered.

I stared. "You think my reality is part of the same simulation YOURS is, though?"

The Doctor stood up and paced, "Oh, I'm positive of it. Especially now."

"Why now?"

"Well, if you think about it, for a simulation to overlap with the real world creating that simulation would be meta-bounding."

La Raza chimed in, "Like if Game of Thrones bled over into the real world and Jon Snow ran for president."

"Got it."

"But, if this reality is also a simulation, then the interaction makes more sense."

Xylocaine stepped in, "Like there is no reason two shows on the same network can't have a crossover."

"Like if 'Always Sunny' and 'Abbot Elementary' had a crossover." La Raza continued.

"Which happened." Zio crossed his arms.

"This is a crossover?"

The doctor said, with authority, "This is a little different, This is the next level. You won the game. You made it…well. Here. What if there was a rule in the game reality that referenced this reality as the 'level' you achieved if you won?"

I tried to take all that in. They all seemed so sure. I had just slumped back into my chair when I saw the little red dot dancing on Zio's forehead. I dove toward the counter but I was too late.

The room erupted into shattered glass, spinning around like a swarm of wasps as Zio's head snapped backward and he fell from his stool. I yelled out, watching everyone else drop to the ground.

"Jesenia!"

She was next to me on the ground, tears welling up in her eyes. "Zio…"

"Ok. I'm sorry, but you have to focus." The room had filled with smoke and dark shapes were stepping over the debris toward us. "I need to get these people out of here."

I was speaking to myself as much as to anyone else. In my head, I tried to place where I had last seen everyone. The Doctor was to my left. On the other side of her was Xylocaine, then Velma. Then the young dark haired girl. I crawled to the Doctor.

She was gone. There was a clean hole in her head, nearly equidistant between her eyes. The rest of these were just kids.

These were kids. They were huddled behind their chairs, staring out.

"Americans," La Raza said, quietly.

"The war was over, you said. The Thousand Islands Treaty…"

"They're right there."

"Could they have come from my reality?"

"I don't know how."

They were advancing in a line, trying to prevent anyone from getting out. This was a common low visibility search technique. The mistake, though, was that it was obvious.

I ducked toward the wall. If I could get parallel, I could make these few bullets work harder. I pulled Jesenia back behind the counter and crawled forward, yelling out once I had reached their level. They stopped and turned. And I let off a stream of shots from the floor, aimed upward and across the line of their bodies. Through the haze, I saw nearly all of them go down. I grabbed a larger piece of glass and wrapped it in my sleeve. Crawling forward, I was able to stab four of them before the ones standing turned and retreated.

"Fearless-17." an amplified voice rang out in front of the store. As the smoke dissipated I could see them. Americans. Lined up between us and the Fearless, still sitting in the parking lot.

Immobile.

"Are they YOUR Americans?" La Raza crouched down next to me as the other three made their way into the back.

I shook my head. I didn't see a drainer on any of them. "No way to tell. Do you have a megaphone, too, here?"

"Yes." She scrambled to grab the battery powered toy from behind the counter and dropped it in my hand.

"All we want is information and you and your friends can go." That was clearly a lie. In negotiations, you only get one.

I lifted the megaphone up. "What about the treaty?"

"The treaty is still in place. This is a stand alone information gathering operation."

These were Americans from this reality. And I was just a famous gamer who had, what? - won the game. I beat the Americans. Ones who were a lot stronger.

Who had futuristic alien allies.

"Get down," I whispered to La Raza. She ducked down and I covered her.

I spoke into the megaphone again. This time louder. "Verte. Cibles devant! Tirez tous."

The Fearless sprung to life. It still didn't have much in terms of weaponry and I couldn't use the turrets, but it fired all of it directly ahead, shearing the line of Americans in two. The sample tube was launched as well, lodging itself into the head of the one standing next to the officer. Those sample tubes were really paying off.

A few bullets made it onto the room. I did my best to protect Jesenia. We both crawled to the counter. "Avant cinquante-cinq mètres."

"It responds to French?"

"Doesn't show you that in the game?"

"It does not."

I held her back, wondering how accurate my guess was. The Fearless pulled up almost directly right next to us. "C'mon." The triage bay was opening right in front of us. I pulled the girl in with me, calling for the others. They ran out from the back room and piled in.

Sliding into the Nav pod, I realized how much more confident I felt in this thing. It didn't matter what reality it was. I spun it around and we powered through the store, making another hole in the outer wall.

"I really loved that place." La Raza was starting to realize what had been lost.

"In the game, I kept going back. Maybe they would come back. The Doctor, Zio..."

"They're dead. In this world, people stay dead." Velma asserted.

"And you are 100% sure of that?"

"My whole life." She wasn't lying.

Zio and the doctor were dead.

And it was my fault.

***

"So, you think the Americans want to find out what you know about how the Americans in the game were winning the war?" La Raza was thinking out loud.

Xylocaine was pacing right outside the Nav pod. "And then restart it?"

"I do. And that is no longer your problem." I looked out at the forest in front of us. Trying to stay off the main roads was costing time.

Jesenia looked at me, "We're in this with you. You can't just drop us off and forget about us"

"Trust me, I'm not forgetting, but you aren't soldiers. I'm not here to get you killed.

'If Americans are invading again, that's the risk no matter what."

I guess Velma wasn't wrong.

She was freaked out, though. I looked over at her.

She looked like she might have been sliding into shock. "Hey. What is your name, anyway? I've been calling you Velma in my head."

She tried to compose herself. "I'm Yani. I don't mind Velma."

"Ok, Yani. It's going to be ok. I have one quick stop and then I need to get you all somewhere safe.

Jesenia whispered to me, "Where ARE we going?"

"If they knew I was there, they know who I am."

"Shit.

***

This time it seemed to take longer, even though we were driving nearly twice as fast. I felt for my gun on my hip as we rounded the corner onto the tree-laden street. I'd gone from hating this stupid piece of metal to touching it randomly just to make sure it was still there. And this time it wasn't going to be big enough.

La Raza pointed, "There."

The door was open, a black smudge in the middle of the red face of the house. And a stream of smoke trailed up from the side window. I drove up onto the lawn and slid out the Nav Bay, running toward the front.

"Mom!" The front room was dark and filled with smoke. I saw a figure on the floor in the kitchen and lowered my gun arm. Her face was covered in blood and her breathing was irregular. There was resignation in her eyes.

"Anaana. Don't move. It's ok. I got you."

"Baby? Tomi?"

"I'm here. I'll get you out of here." I put my hand behind her head to lift and felt the warm wet sludge. There was a hole in her head where someone had crushed it with an object.

"Oh, mom."

"No. baby. You're up? That's good. I knew. I always knew."

Her eyes were glazing over, a layer of white over their onyx blackness. "Anguta qaujip"

I put my forehead up against hers. "He is. It's ok. He's here."

"Is he pretty?"

"He's so handsome."

"I knew he'd be pretty."

"You did."

"You're my pretty, too. And you're all healed, now."

"I am. Anaanaapiingai. You can go."

"You were always so beautiful. Nagliga."

I held her while she died, pretending to be her daughter. The last thing she saw was a lie.

And that was one more thing someone had to pay for.

The smoke was slowly worsening as I moved into the back room. The Americans had stripped it, taking every piece of technology, every part of the game they could.

There was nothing left.

Through the gauze, I could see the real Tomi Pinga, one eye still looking out like a perfect black glass marble in its white nest. I reached into the drawer next to the bed and quickly searched for what I needed.

I pulled out the three bottles and filled the syringe, one after another. Full to the top, I placed the tip of the syringe against the bicep of her last remaining arm. I looked into her face for some sign of assent, some symbol that I was doing the right thing.

But there was nothing. We were the same person but I didn't have what it took to get through to her. I thought about how many people I had killed today and let the syringe fall into her skin as through quicksand, quickly giving the plunger one pump.

It hit me.

Eighteen months in the past. Where WAS I from? What was the date here, now, in this simulation? This was me.

I wrapped my hands around her fingerless hand and held her eye's gaze as long as I could. I wanted to be there, in her line of sight, as long as possible. I knew how bizarre all of this must have been to her. I cried as her eye closed and held onto her hand until it went cold.

I think part of me expected myself to disappear as she died. Part of me thought that I was connected to her like that and I would fade away, maybe that all of this would fade away.

But there I was. Still.

The fire was smoldering. It looked like the Americans had started it, trying to cover up the evidence, and it had burnt out. These buildings were old growth wood, thick and multi-layered. It would take more than a hasty half assed torch to burn it down.

I moved into the kitchen and wet the towels and aprons hanging from the back of the door. I moved back into the back room and spread them across the floor, pouring more water over all of it.

The smoldering carpet seemed to have died down. I looked at the mess of a room and a tiny voice in the back of my head reminded me that my fastidious mother would hate this so much.

***

La Raza was leaning against the ship as I left the house. I moved slowly to where she stood and looked down at the grass. I had basically destroyed the lawn driving this massive machine up on it. Another thing my mom would have hated. I kicked at the tufts of grass ripped up. Once I moved the Fearless, I could come back and roll these tracks back out, patting the grass down. I was sure I could make it so that you would never even notice the tracks.

The girl next to me hugged me tightly and I hugged her back. In that moment, she seemed a little older. We fell back against the Fearless, leaning next to each other.

"Do you need anything?"

I reached in my pocket. I knew it was still there. I had stolen it last time I was here. The little USB thumb drive felt so light in my hand, so inconsequential.

"Yes. I do." I placed the drive in her hand.

"And you're going to help me get everything we need."

17 - La Raza

"Colonel, is that you?"

I felt like I hadn't heard Rey's voice in forever. And as much as I missed it, there were others I missed. "It is. Rey, it's good to hear from you. Is everything ok?"

I held my breath. When I closed my eyes, the grief spun around in my head. There was a pit opening in front of me. I prepared myself to fall into it.

"We're all fine, too, doofus, where are you?"

It was Ladia. It felt like I was sitting in a car that suddenly shot into reverse. I put my hands on the table to steady myself. We had made some changes - started the game further back. I didn't believe that this was possible. "And Ella....Filo?"

Hearing Ladia's voice filled me up. And Ella laughing in the background, too. "I'm ok. And smartypants is fine, too. Where the hell did you go?"

I heard Filo's laugh. This was real. They were there, in the game.

Suddenly, I was ready to do this. All my doubts were washed away.

"That is really complicated. But I'm good and I need you guys to join me."

"Yes, absolutely, Colonel. If you give us directions, we'll be there asap."

Rey sounded relieved as well. I hoped they hadn't been through too much. Just enough to do what was needed. I gave thanks for everything that was washed away. Everything that wouldn't happen.

"It's not as easy as that. Do you still have the unnamed ship? The Green one?"

"Yep, it's all cleaned up now and looking good." Filo sounded ready for all this.

Let's see how ready they were.

Ok. I'm sending the coordinates to the Braca hotel. And we..." I looked over at Jesenia, who was still uploading on her gamer laptop. "We are sending you a video of exactly what you have to do."

Rey came back on, "I don't understand, Colonel. What we have to do?"

"This is really a little complex. Think of it as an exercise. One we have to execute exactly. You will see video of how I did it. You have to do it exactly like I did."

"Understood."

For not the first time, I appreciated Rey's impeccable British manner. He didn't understand it, but he would do it. I knew that. That was the subtle genius of Rey. He trusted the process. He was willing to put the work in for it.

"Ok, I'll be in touch consistently on this channel until we're together again."

"You better be, man." Ladia signed off.

I reached down and put my hand on the speaker, imagining that she could feel it on the other side. The room was dancing with light filtered through the water in my eyes. I couldn't catch my breath. I imagined her warm cheek on my palm and I could barely stand it. The other side.

But the other side of what? I breathed in. "It's really all of them, isn't it?"

"For them, I could start the game anywhere, with any parameters."

"Thank you, Jesenia."

"It's La Raza when I'm doing this shit."

"Ok, La Raza, the iteration of the game from my home server seems like it's running perfectly. And you have the videos packaged."

"I do."

"And I appreciate you keeping all those. We have the exact blueprint of how I got to this level."

"I started up the other iterations." Her fingers flew over the keyboard. "And modded the one I already had started."

I looked over her shoulder. There was a version of Zio and Dr. Kinley on her crew. I put my hand on her shoulder and she put hers over it. We'd developed an understanding in a remarkably short period of time. For such a young girl, she 'got' a lot. I realized that she started playing this game for the same reason I started in the military.

To help people. It made her happy. Even the illusion of it.

On one level, we'd learned, it didn't matter if they were real or not. The line between people and simulations of people was getting progressively thinner.

Until it had just washed away. The feeling was the same. and it was good. It's just how we're made, humans.

I looked around the room, "It's kind of spooky how much these stores look alike. Or looked."

"Yep. Exactly the same. Except it's about thirty minutes away. Welcome to Orleans. Gamezetera 2."

"Wait. I thought the one in Ottowa was number 2."

"Nope. This is just the one Zio came from originally.

So he called it number one and that one number 2. In reality, the Ottawa location opened first. Regardless, the owners are pretty cool.

"The reason why that first version of the game the other me played was so robust was that it was played so fast, right, modded?"

"Oh, we modded these, too. Plus..." she motioned to me. We walked out to the main floor. There were four rows of tables lined up. Sitting at them, with their gaming computers, must have been almost a hundred young gamers. All of them playing the game. Two slightly older men sat on the end, equally immersed. Jesenia pointed. "And those are the owners."

"Damn."

"They're sending out for more computers now. I know I have more people."

"For the war effort, huh?"

"Yup. I don't know how many of them really believe it's real, but they're on it."

"They don't believe it's real? But they're helping anyway?" I knew I was acting giddy. And I didn't care. The world had delivered so much pain. But today it gave back.

"What's the alternative?" Jesenia looked sad. She knew what it would mean if we lost.

"Ok. Come here." I grabbed her hand.

***

"I will never get used to how cool this is." She ran after me through the Triage Zone.

"I can't believe you never asked about the coolest thing on the whole ship."

I made my way through the central corridor and made a beeline to the aggregator in the kitchen area.

"No fucking way. That can't work here?"

"Didn't you hear Dr. Kinley? This reality is a simulation, too. It's not all that dissimilar to the one I come from. I placed my hand on the front screen on the aggregator and began typing.

"What are you doing?"

"I'm bringing a little reality to the situation. Grab me a bag from under that shelf."

"You are a crazy person, but I like it."

I realized that I had been treating all of this with kid gloves, playing by rules I thought I needed to play by. But none of that was necessary, was it? This was real. All of it. The implications of all of it were explosive. Ladia was alive. Filo was alive. I just heard their voices. This was a reality. Even if it wasn't one I was used to. I was in a different universe on the brink of a whole new war. And this one would kill even more people than the last. If we couldn't stop it.

In the store behind us were all those kids, doing their parts. And even the owners of the place, lining up to help, after their other store was shot to shit. It was time to pull out all the stops.

It was time to stop playing by their rules.

"Yeah, Grab a few of those bags."

***

Back in the store, La Raza and I dumped three bags out in the middle of the tables. They were full of bundles of cash.

Altogether, replicated on the aggregator, four hundred tightly wrapped bundles of 10,000 dollars each, Canadian.

Four Million Dollars.

"Ok. For anything needed. Everyone, take a few. If we get split up or if anything bad happens, feel free to buy your way out of any problems. Literally, throw money at shit." I watched them stare as I addressed the owners.

"And there's more coming for you both for the other store."

The taller one, with brown hair and a moustache, was named Pierre. He stood up and nodded. "I don't really care about that. We just got to make sure we keep these kids safe."

"That's what the other bags are for."

Jesenia poured one of the other bags out on a nearby table. It was full of small black Tasers.

"And we're all going to take turns learning how to use these things."

***

"Between you and me, I have thirty thousand dollars in my bra," Yani shot the Taser at a tree in the back, behind the store.

"I thought you were looking a little bustier. Nice shot. Imma call you center mass from now on." Velma had some chops, I thought.

"Fuck that tree." La Raza was helping Claire, the young short-haired girl, aim.

Claire spoke up, "So, who's the prime minister in that other reality?"

That was a good question. I tried to remember.

I'm a reasonably political person, aren't I? I would have known that. But it wasn't part of the character profile or the world builder specs.

"I don't know." I'm sure I looked confused.

Xylocaine was trying to practice drawing the tasers, two of them, from a holster around his waist that I think he already had. "So we have to be really thorough with the character builders here."

La Raza agreed, "I mean, in essence, we're making real people."

This was just another thing I may not have considered. And that worried me. The version of me in the game, the one I was used to being, that version didn't miss things. That version didn't make big mistakes or have giant blind spots.

That version I trusted.

Xylocaine fell over and I dove over him to deactivate the taser. I figured someone would shoot themselves. He just won the pool.

Piere ran out of the back door and helped me lift Xylocaine onto a picnic table. He would be fine. He motioned me to come with him.

"Hey, You probably want to come see this."

***

The other ship seemed even bigger than the Fearless. It was cleaned off, but otherwise, just as I'd seen it last. Green pods where the Fearless had safety yellow. But otherwise identical. ATARAS-31. Unnamed. There was smoke rising from the ground where the tank tires touched and a kind of heaviness, a weight, that threatened to compress the asphalt of the lot under its twin tracks.

It sat in the parking lot facing my right. No one had seen it appear, it just… was.

The Triage bay opened and She stepped out. It was her.

It was Ladia.

She saw me, standing next to Pierre and the others. She walked over and wrapped her arms around me, falling into me. We struggled to see which one would crush the other one as I buried my face in her neck. My eyes filled up. I was prepared. I had promised myself.

I felt the rest wrap around me. Ella, Symone, Rey, and finally Filo. His arms were strong and they seemed to pull us all together. I slipped my hand around and grabbed his fingers. They were warm and alive.

Alive.

All of them.

Here.

***

Rey, Filo, and Symone stayed to work with the gamers. It was probably the strangest briefing of my life, but there was no avoiding what the truth was. The world that we thought of as real was no more real than any other game off the shelf. And this world?

It made my brain hurt. But I had no choice but to believe it.

Rey worked with them on self-defense, while Filo and Jesenia worked out the final details of the plan. It required that we go all in, believing what the evidence was trying to tell us. In a way, we were "hacking" this universe and the one below in ways that should never work.

But they were.

I wondered what would happen if everyone really understood what This Bostrom guy was saying.

As a people, we struggle to treat each other well, even when we think we are all real. What happens when we have iron clad proof - not just vague mathematical proof, that all this is a simulation. How would we treat each other then? Would everything just fall apart? It reminded me that "I think, therefore I am" wasn't going to be good enough. We were going to have to be things that felt, things that cared. We were going to have to fight for empathy the way we were willing to fight for ourselves. Or these simulations would be devoid of anything real.

There would BE no people anymore.

***

It didn't take long for Ladia and Ella to get familiar with the inside of the Fearless again. It didn't hurt that the ATAs were all alike. It did, however, take a lot of research to hunt the section down. Beechwood military cemetary was big, bigger than it should have been. And it had expanded during the war. That last part hurt to think about. The people who propose wars are never the ones who really suffer from them.

"Yours isn't here." Ella stepped back after searching the immediate area.

"Nope. I survived the crash. I just died a few days ago." I closed my eyes and tried not to consider the implications of what I was saying.

"I know there's a story there." Ladia looked over at me.

I sighed. "I barely made it. I was a mess." I held Ella's hand and told them what had happened - the things that I had skipped in my briefing.

"Well. You should be right there." Ladia pointed to a spot right in between her and Herman. Ella was buried right behind.

"That seems kind of cramped." They probably would have had to bury me sideways.

"That's it, though. That's all we got for you. That tiny little space for your skinny butt. Hold on." Ladia took a flower and placed it in the little area between. "You SO skinny."

I shrugged. It seemed little, sitting there, but I'd take it.

"I wish Herman could have been here."

Ella squeezed my hand tighter. "Hey, remember Wyclos? That guy from basic?"

Ladia continued, "How about Shimmy? From Ionia." suddenly her face popped into my head, strong, clear, like she was standing right there.

I sighed. "I remember Martia, that cute girl from Ionia."

Ladia smiled. I remembered the name of the girl that she had hooked up with.

And when we stopped laughing it was so quiet you could hear the wind wrap around the trees working impossibly hard just to rustle one or two leaves for just a moment before moving on, trying with all its might to change the world in its path, to be something more than an invisible gust of air.

**

I can't tell you, today, how that first war began. I have a strange and sometimes conflicting aggregation of what this world's version of me programmed into her character generator and what I'd learned since. But no matter what, it seemed to ramp up faster here this time. There was no bluff and bravado. The first time, America's president had spent almost a year on language meant to make people believe that they had a right to the country. This was language that positioned Canada as a failed country that was endangering the US through its proximity.

Sure, it was all lies, but most of his administration was.

By the time they invaded the first time, they'd done their best to convince people that it HAD to happen for US security. They had no choice.

They had no choice but to turn the largest friendly border between two countries into a nightmare of murder and chaos. No choice but to overturn the lives of tens of millions of people on a pissing game, just because the idea of HAVING a border in the first place triggered them.

This time, there were no words. There were no press conferences or indications that the Thousand Island Treaty had been broken. There was nothing to alert the French or the British or any of our other Allies that they would be needed again.

There was just subterfuge and assassinations in the middle of the night. There was seeding the water with technology, spawned in the future, that left it toxic for living things. There were bombs, built from the bodies of monsters, triggered by heartbeats and movement, ripping apart people, turning civilians into casualties and clearing border towns for the relentless drive of American tanks, the seemingly unstoppable pressure of American technology.

And there were zombies and plaguebringers and giant insects, rats, and fish - more things that this reality wasn't ready for - derived from a twisted America in a simulated world, one that had become, overnight, a tainted, diseased tributary that bled into this one. Our team had been working on building an army to bring to this reality. And it looked like theirs had, too. And like before, maybe we weren't prepared for the brutality of what that meant to them.

But this time, Canada responded quickly. It didn't waste time in nostalgic negotiations, remembering what used to be true, or in efforts to appease a monolith that seemed to have no reason or interest in peace.

It rallied. And we were a part of that. And as we stood on the border, everything that had happened before clarified what we were doing, and why it was important.

And maybe it was a taser and a crovel on my belt this time, and not a gun, but that was a personal preference more than anything.

I was there to do my job. And so was everyone else.

I handed the binoculars to Jesenia. "Take a look."

As we stood there, looking north, the dark wave became more clear. It was a massive throng of zombies moving forward, with fast, jerky motions, unthinking, each more terrifyingly torn and emaciated than the one before, the older ones with tentacles reaching from their mouths all the way to the ground, each with raw, ragged rips down their faces revealing a rapacious maw full of steel tipped teeth.

"Holy fuck."

"Keep watching." I pointed her toward the right flank. I'd seen it. As she looked, one of the zombies fluttered and flickered out of existence, like a faulty hologram, or a flame on a candle, extinguished.

"Is that?"

"Your virus. Your computer virus to counter the biological one."

"What the fuck did I do?"

I looked over at her. "You won the war. Again. They just don't know it yet."

Behind me, over a hundred nearly identical versions of the Fearless rose up over the wooded embankment - filled with teams generated by a group of teenagers sitting around a table in a retail video game store.

Ella stepped around from the side handing me a communicator.

It was Rey. "We're headed out, Colonel. Are we cleared?"

I let his voice wash over me and smiled. "Affirmative, Fearless. We are coordinated. Good to go, Rey."

"Excellent."

Ella answered, "La Raza out."

Jesenia fingered the name smoothly silkscreened on the side of the ship before we piled in, one at a time, through the Nav Bay - The newly painted words a daily reminder of what all this was about - not land or levels or money, or any of that.

And we moved forward.

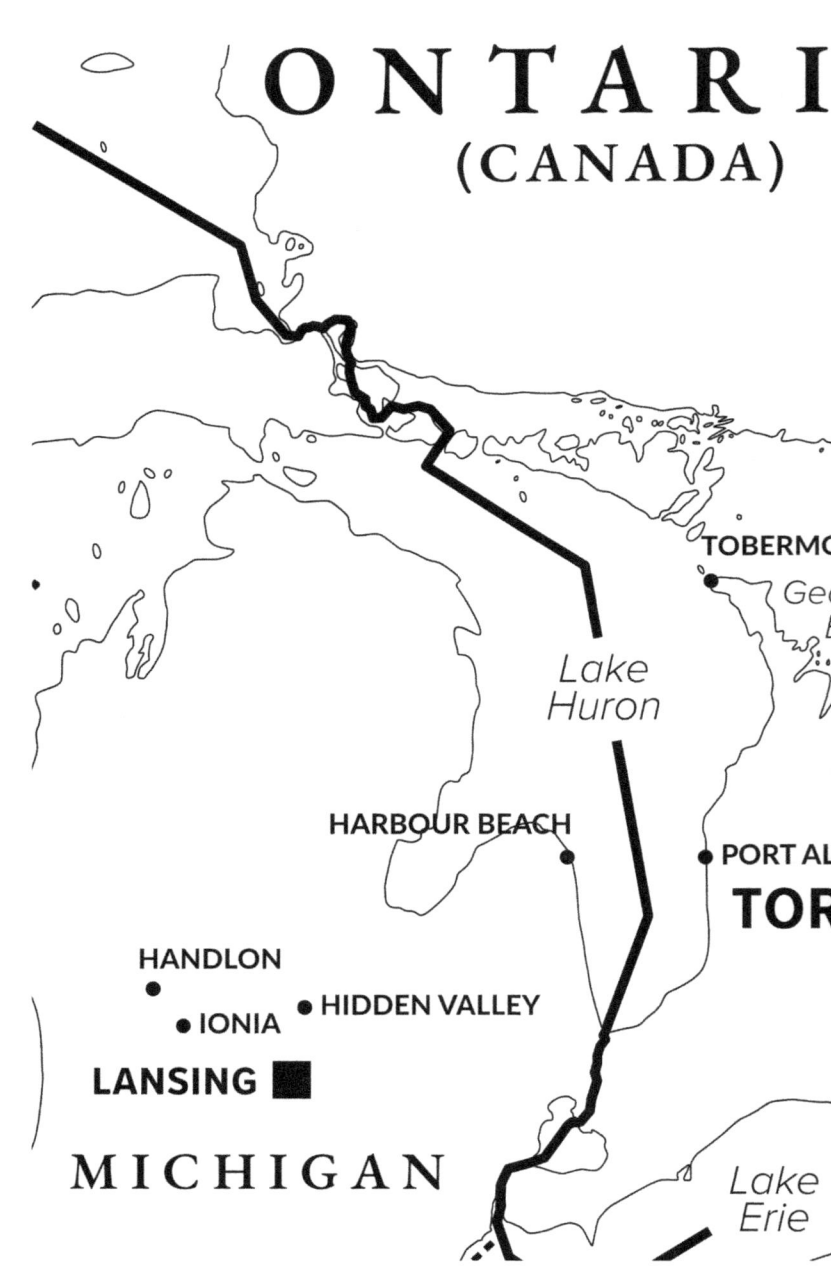

by XENOX®

OTTAWA ■

• WAASEYAAGMIING

• HOTEL BRACA

TO ■

N E W

Y O R

• Rochester

ALBA

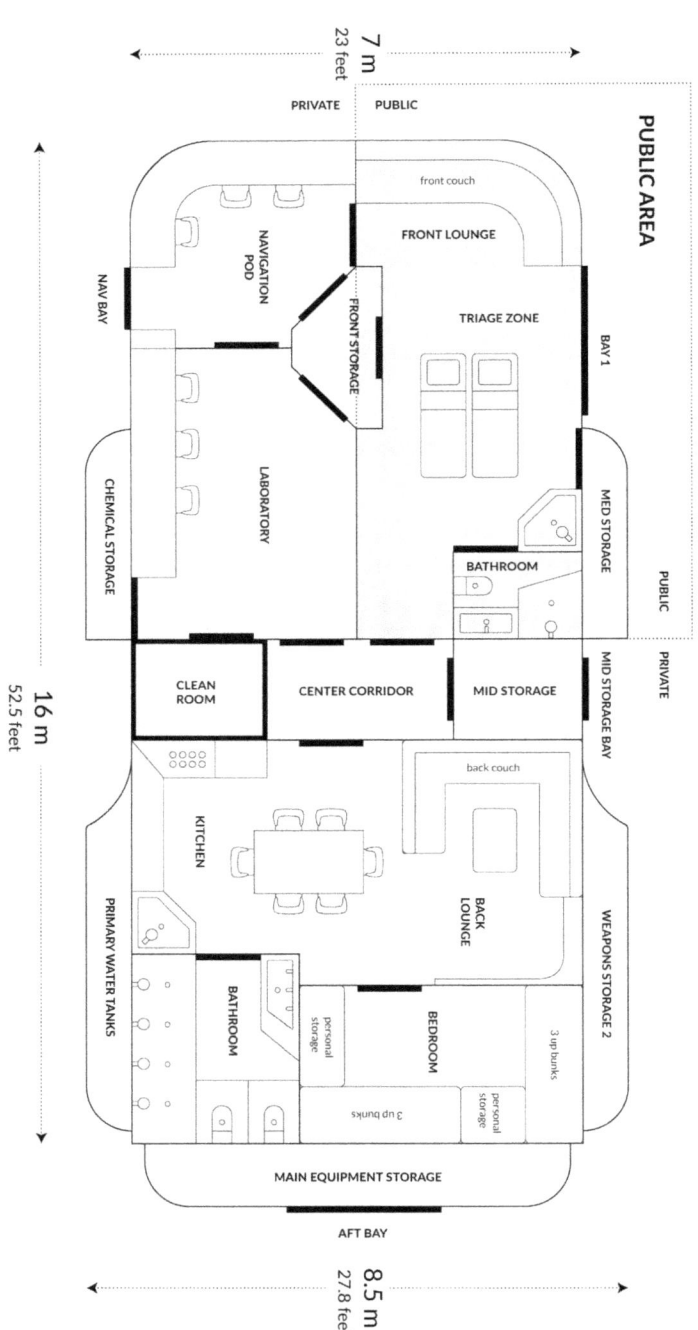

FEARLESS-17

7 m
23 feet

PRIVATE | PUBLIC

PUBLIC AREA

front couch

FRONT LOUNGE

NAVIGATION POD

NAV BAY

FRONT STORAGE

TRIAGE ZONE

BAY 1

LABORATORY

CHEMICAL STORAGE

MED STORAGE

BATHROOM

PUBLIC

PRIVATE

16 m
52.5 feet

CLEAN ROOM

CENTER CORRIDOR

MID STORAGE

MID STORAGE BAY

KITCHEN

back couch

BACK LOUNGE

WEAPONS STORAGE 2

PRIMARY WATER TANKS

BATHROOM

personal storage

BEDROOM

3 up bunks

personal storage

3 up bunks

MAIN EQUIPMENT STORAGE

AFT BAY

8.5 m
27.8 feet

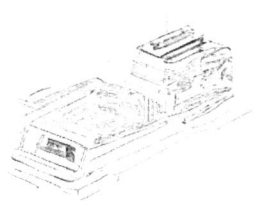

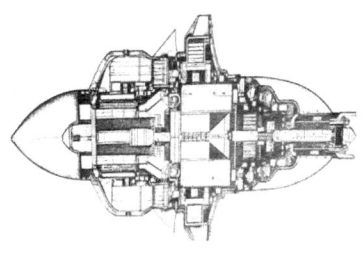

CHASSIS ASSEMBLY

LOWER TANK ASSEMBLY

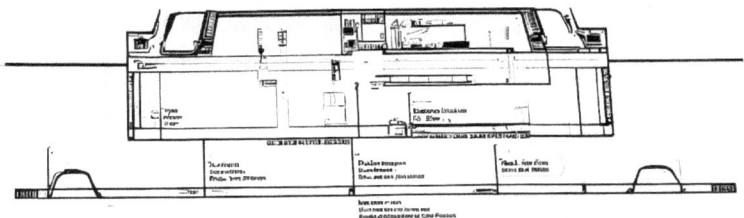

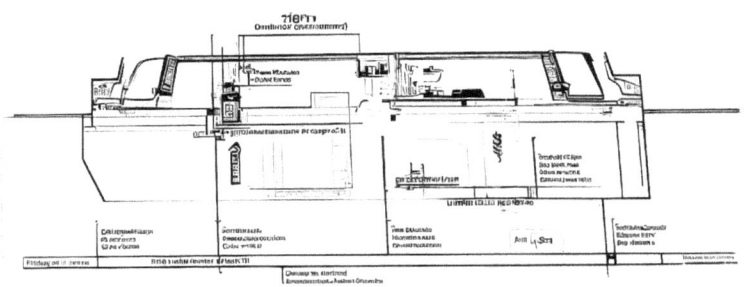

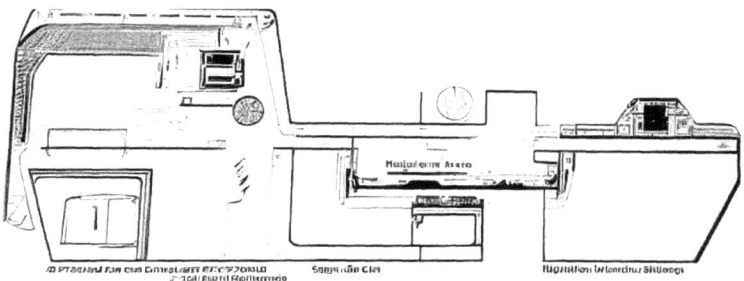

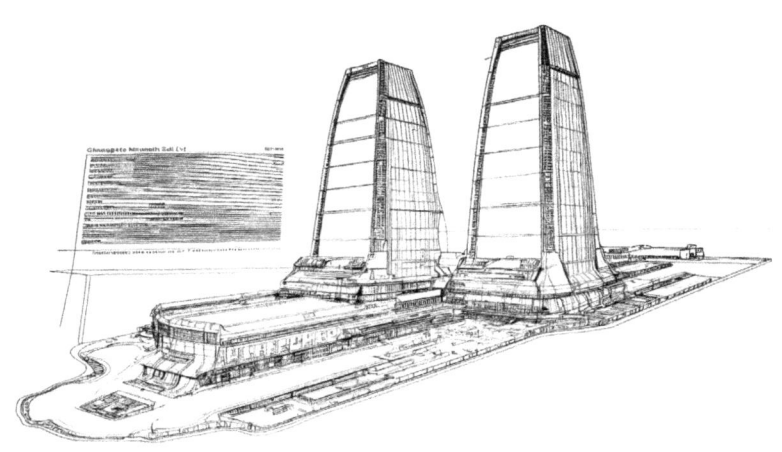

IONIA

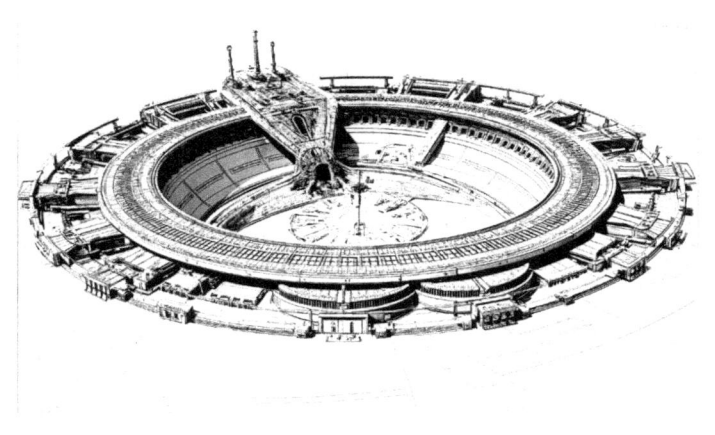

PORT ALBERT

AGGREGATOR CORE

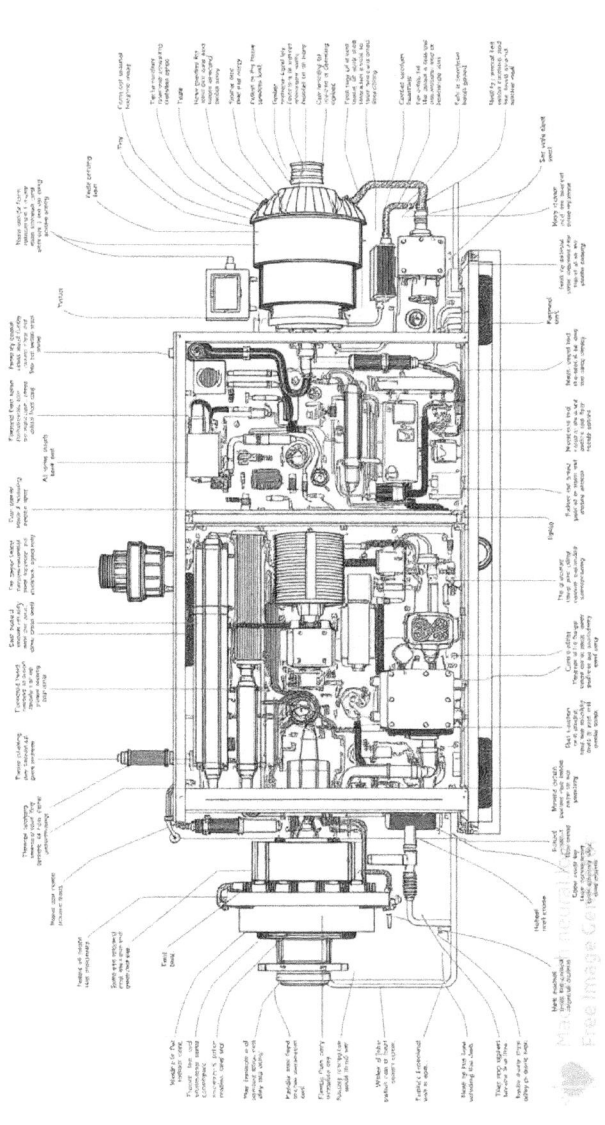

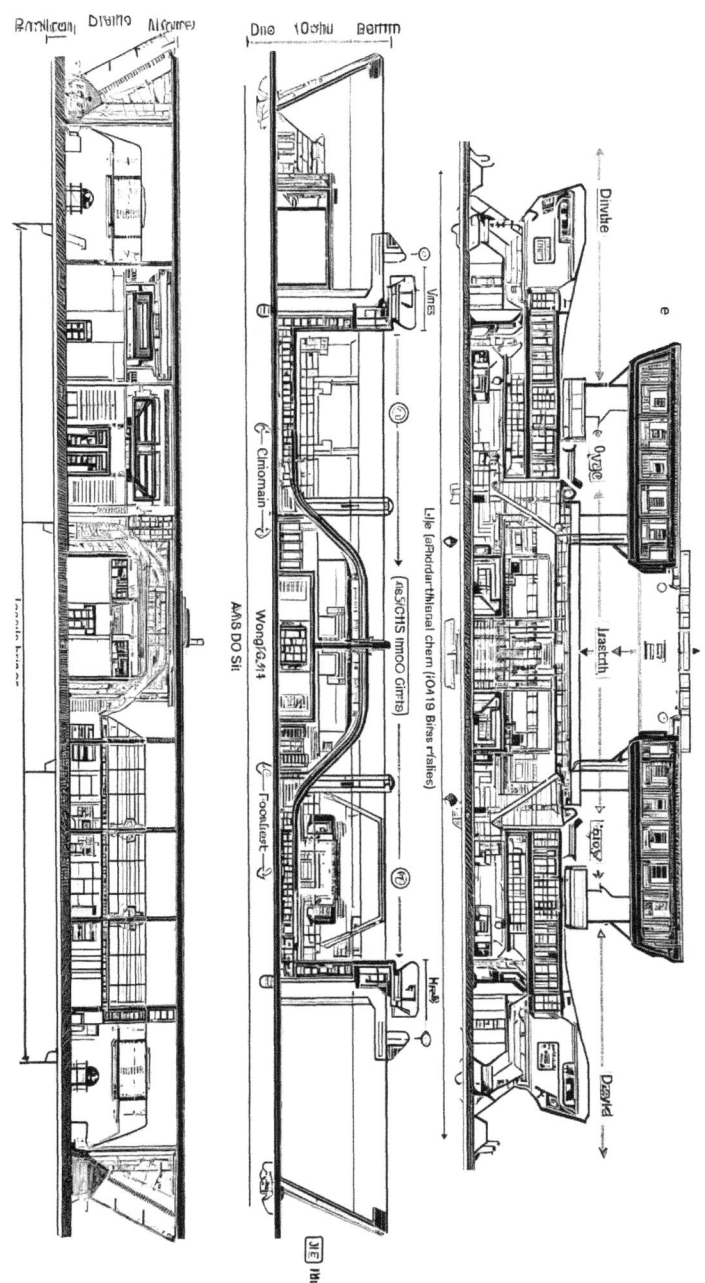

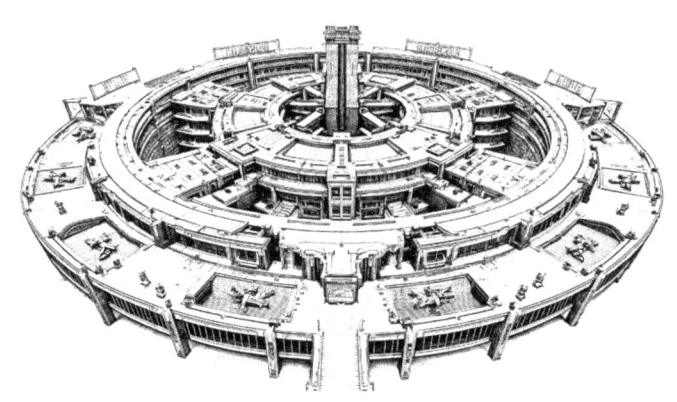

TOBERMOREY

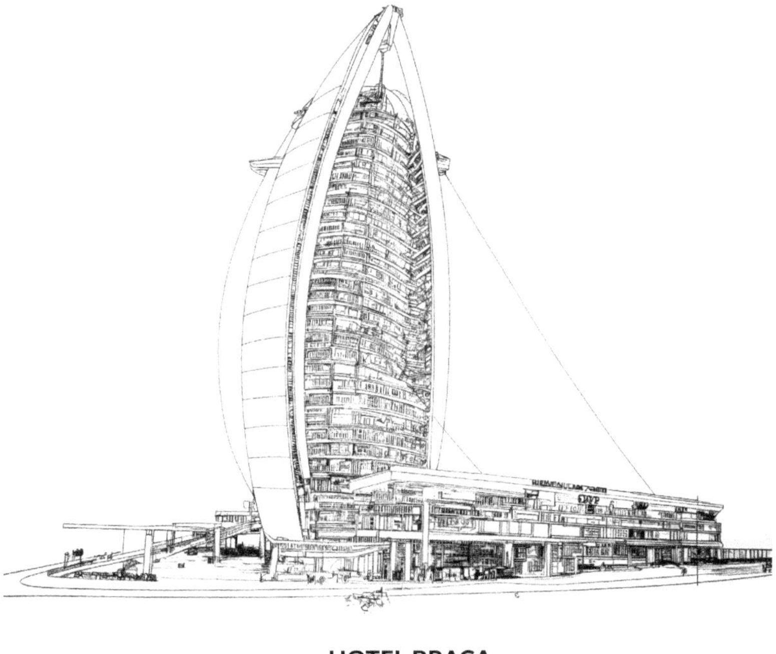

HOTEL BRACA